Growing up i choice but to know someone that worked in the automotive industry. We have this thing called the Big 3, which includes, Chrysler, Ford, and GM. There are many other smaller plants across the state, but these 3 companies make up the majority of workers in the field. Over my first three years, I encountered many people and even met a few people that work at different facilities. After hearing so many stories about the experiences at my location and many others, I decided to write a book bringing to the rest of the world this thing we call Plant Life. I sat down with three different people from three different facilities and took some examples of their experiences, along with some things I've seen myself and came up with this masterpiece. Oh yeah, some names have been changed to protect the innocent, and this is just entertainment. These are not true events, just examples of how some things happen in this Plant Life. So kick back, and enjoy!

Omari "O" Bonner

NAME LIST

TJ = ALWAYS HURT

MICHELLE = 2ND SUPERVISOR

KAREN = CO-WORKER

VICKIE = KAREN'S FRIEND

PAUL = 1ST STEWARD

DON P = 1ST SUPERVISOR

LARRY = 1ST TL

MASON = ME (MASE)

TOYA = CO-WORKER

JP = MACK'S BOY

KAMESHA = ALWAYS HURT

TOM = CO-WORKER

SARAH = GIRLFRIEND

CED = 2ND TL

MACK = HOMEBOY, CO-WROKER

H = OLD SCHOOL PLAYER

JAZZ = COWORKER

PAULINE'S = LOCAL BAR

NEW BEGINNING

Buzz, buzz, buzz…. Buzz, buzz, buzz."Damn", I say to myself, another job. It's been two years since I was laid-off from my last job and I'm finally starting the next chapter in my life. I'm glad I'm back in the workforce but kind of nervous to be beginning this chapter in the auto industry. I worked in the custodial field for most of my life so working in a plant will be new to me. Well I've worked in a few plants but nothing at this scale or level.

Today is my first day at Jefferson North Assembly Plant in the paint shop. I had a few friends and relatives retire from the company so I've heard stories firsthand on how it is to work in a big plant atmosphere. They tried to tell us what to expect in orientation but I'm sure it's not as simple as they make it seem. This is also the first time I've been in a union, meaning there is a slight barrier between an employee and management. Being a part of a union allows one to have a voice in the workplace and actually have somewhat of a say so when it comes to wages, hours, benefits, and other work-related issues.

The automotive business has had its ups and downs over the years, lastly being the major buyouts and layoffs that happened only a few years before. That is certainly something I had to take into consideration before I decided to accept this employment offer. Not to mention that I just graduated with my Associates degree in Surgical Technology.

As I pull into the parking lot a slight sense of nervousness comes over me. Not because I'm actually nervous, but just the fact of starting something new in a field that I've only heard about but never experienced. It is a workplace that can be very beneficial but also a curse at the same time.

I wasn't offered a full-time position at first but a TPT position which means Temporary Part Time. I was hesitant in accepting that because I was looking for full-time work, but until I start my healthcare career, I'll work this in the meantime. Yes, I said healthcare. I've worked in the ER at a main hospital in housekeeping for three years, while attending Wayne County Community College, majoring in Surgical Technology. Graduated just last week and *this* week I'm working in a plant. Crazy, I know. I couldn't sit back and wait on the future money though.

When I first walk in the plant I immediately think about all the key points the union members stressed in orientation. No headphones, no radios, and safety comes first. The first thing I see when I notice an employee? Some damn earbuds stuck in her ear. I laugh to myself and nudge a young lady walking with my group as we go on our plant tour. "You see that shit?" I ask. "I guess the rules only apply to the new people." The tour guide/union member takes each person to the area where they will be working and somehow, I end up in one of the easiest areas. The very first thing someone says before anything else is "don't get used to it youngblood, you gotta put your time in to get back here." I laugh to myself thinking, yeah, ok, I really don't give a shit anyway. As soon as I get my first hospital offer, I'm probably taking it.

They give us these blue jumpsuits that we're supposed to wear every day, which is good because I usually don't have any "work clothes", only old clothes that I can wear. A few ladies jokingly tell me that some people wear only underwear under their jumpsuit. I think about that and visualize the thought at the same time and tuck that away in my mental pocket. I'm definitely just not wearing my underwear up in here. After I get my jumpsuit on and come back to the floor, it's hard not imagining and wondering if any, out of all the ladies working here is actually *only* wearing underwear under their jumpsuit. Yeah, crazy, I know, but the thought was already put in my head, I didn't just put it there

Like I said before, I was hired as a TPT, temporary part-time worker. This means I am usually required to work Friday, Saturday, and Monday. Any other days are extra. I have to call this number on Thursdays to get my weekly schedule, but any extra time or days can be approved by a supervisor. Every area has its own UL, or supervisor, to make sure everything is running how it should be. When I say running, I'm referring to the line that carries the carriages with the vehicles that are being manufactured and assembled by the workers. The UL has a boss that is over their assigned area and that person is the bull, spelled BUL. The BUL oversees the UL, and the UL oversees the team leaders, or TL's. What is a team leader? What does a team leader do, and what role do they play in the whole plant process? A team leader is someone who provides guidance, instruction, direction, and leadership to a group of individuals for a purpose of achieving a key result or results. Now let all that sink in and we'll get back to that on a few occasions.

After having a quick little huddle about the objectives for the day, we are led to the specific area where we will be reporting. My supervisor introduces himself as Don P and informs us that his other guy standing towards the back is the TL, Larry. Larry doesn't even say shit, he just does a quick wave to let people know who he is. Now, I've never been one to judge a book by its cover, but when I notice his clothes, I notice they look damn near new! Once again, maybe he just put it on fresh out the pack, but whatever the case, his uniform doesn't appear as if it belongs to someone who works in a plant. He has a look of someone who just sits back and goes through the motions. When I think of plant work, and all the experience I've had in smaller plants in the past, he *definitely* doesn't appear as a grit and grind worker. I would expect to see *some* type of oil stain or something on his jumpsuit but nope, his shit looks like he just took it out the pack. Like I said before, he could have just opened it or washed it, but his whole demeanor is saying otherwise.

After the little huddle, Larry comes over and tells me and this other young lady to come with him so he can show us where we will be working. We get to this small machine that he say is used to make sure the right color is put on each vehicle. It requires this container full of tubes to be loaded in and then you press a button for the rest of the process. Only thing that's really work is walking to get the parts to be loaded. That's simple. I'm thinking one person can probably do all this by themselves but, oh well, I just work here. After Larry walks off I quickly tell the young lady that she can sit back and run the machine and I'll go and get the parts as needed. "How you know I didn't want to go get the parts?" She quickly says. "Well I just figured you would want to sit back and chill on the easy stuff", I quickly stated. "I didn't know you wanted to do the *work* part of the job. My bad!" She could see that I was smiling so she just jumped right back saying "you know what, you can get the parts though. I was just playing." "Ok, no more changes", I said laughing. "Or you gone be doing all the work. Getting *and* loading the parts."

About an hour after we had started working, she stopped me as I was dropping off her parts. "Wait, you didn't even tell me your name." "Mason", I said. "Everybody call me Mase though." "Okay, M-A dollar sign", she joked. "And yours?" I asked. "Shatoya", she replied. "So, no nickname or nothing?" I asked. "I mean, some people call me Toya, but that's about it." "Okay, Toya it is", I said. "What did you do before you started here?" "I worked for DTE in the call center", she said. "And no, I wasn't cutting people shit off either, I was the one trying to keep people shit *on*." "Ummhmm", I say. "So you were part of the solution. You still probably got cussed out a few times." "You already know", she said, as we both laughed.

We could see Larry from where she was working, sitting at his desk, reading a magazine. It must be nice to be able to get paid to read the ESPN magazine. I'm not sure what he should be doing or when he has to actually work, but he hasn't done shit but sit at his desk since we came over here. I can't really complain though because my day is easy anyway. It' not like I'm sweating or nothing, even in this jumpsuit.

A bell rings and I guess it's the bell that signals break time because people start moving and shifting at a somewhat fast pace going wherever. Larry comes over and says its break time and we have thirteen minutes until we have to be back at our work station. What kind of odd ass number is that? Thirteen minutes? Whatever. Let me find the bathroom before this break is over. I'm definitely not coming back late on my first day. I ask a guy walking in the area where the restroom is at and he points in the direction of the food truck. I can see a group of people gathering over by the truck so I decide to stop and see what the lady is selling. She has a lot of breakfast sandwiches and breakfast meals already prepared so I find one with French toast on it and decide to try it out. I didn't eat breakfast today so this right-on time. I notice the line is a little long so I do a time check and see that I have eight minutes left before the break is over. The lady is moving as fast as she can but it's still seeming like the process is taking forever. I'm steadily looking at my phone and looking at the truck lady like "damn, hurry up". I whispered to myself what the fuck and I guess the lady behind me could hear me, because she says "I know, right. We only got thirteen minutes and that shit turns to ten immediately after the bell rings. This shit crazy". We both laugh at the bullshit and shake our heads while waiting on our turn. After I finally reach the front and pay, I check my watch and it says 8:09. So, I basically have wasted my break for some French toast I guess. The more I think about it, French toast is my favorite so it's not a waste. I'll just ask Larry to use the restroom after I finish my food. Its not like he just super busy so he shouldn't have a problem with it. The truck should stay longer really. I mean thirteen minutes for a break is like seven when you put a quick bathroom visit in it, or *any* visit in it. Its like you have a choice, either food or restroom.

I'm walking back towards my work area and I can see Toya standing talking to some other young lady and before I can even get there I hear her yelling "oh, for real though"! I'm felling puzzled because I don't even know what she is talking about, so when I get over there I ask, "what you mean"? semi-smiling. She immediately starts going off in a jokingly manner. "So you just gone go get you a breakfast and not even bring a bitch a biscuit, bagel, sausage or nothing huh? You ain't even say you was going to the lunch truck. How the hell you even *find* the lunch truck?" "Well", I said, "I was actually on my way to the bathroom and when I saw the truck I got detoured. Shit, I was already thinking about what I was gone eat for lunch, so when I saw that, it was perfect." "Yeah, whatever", she said. "You should've brought me something anyway." I'm laughing but I'm feeling sort of guilty. "You eat French toast?" I ask. She quickly answers "no, I eat pancakes. But today I'll gladly take a piece of French toast." She then walks up and opens her mouth saying, "feed it to me." I use the fork and let her take a bite off one of the pieces. "Here, I'm not about to feed you", I say as I leave the fork in the container. "I can't even believe I'm being this nice, let alone letting you eat off my fork. I don't know *where* you mouth has been. You might be wild as hell. Shit, you already ate off my fork on the first day." Toya is looking shocked at this point. "My mouth ain't been nowhere actually", she said. "At least recently. I been solo for almost a year so I know where my mouth been." "I hear you", I say, smiling. "But you not ugly in no way so I'm sure dudes be all on your head." "That don't mean anything", she says. "You can't just go for all the bullshit you hear. It's a lot of bullshit in the air and I'm not trying to breathe none of that shit."

    The other young lady had been sitting there the whole time on a cart listening and laughing to the conversation. I turn to her and tell her the job must be real gravy for her to be able to chill the way she is. The bell rings and she didn't even budge. "My route is stocked up already, and plus I need to come check on my cousin and make sure she good. And for your info, it took me two years to get this tugger job, so I put my time in to be able to relax like this." "Alrighty then", I say. "At least you admitting you chilling and not working hard. Your cousin on the same shit too, though, just without a cart. So ya'll keeping it in the family. Why you think she got so much time to talk? I'm doing all the hard work and I told her she can just kick back." "So, you like my cousin or something?" she asks. "You must've saw her fat ass before she put that jumpsuit on." I can't even hold the laughter in at this point. "I haven't even *seen* your cousin outside this work area, so it's no way I could know what she got back there. I mean, I can see it through the jumpsuit, but I can't *see it*! Plus, I haven't really looked at her like that anyway." "So, you telling me you haven't noticed that big ass she got? Okay. I told her she can give me some of that shit to fill my shit out." "You crazy", I say, laughing. "Thank for putting me up on it though. I guess you learn something every day for real."

    Toya had already started working while me and her cousin were talking, so I finished and went over and told her I would talk some more with her when I came back. I also still need to go to the restroom since I didn't make it on the last break. I guess I'll work a little bit and then ask my TL Larry could he cover me while I make a quick bathroom run. I think I saw him going to the lunch truck so I'll give him a few minutes before I hit him with the bathroom break. I'm pretty sure he not busy, especially since all the jobs on his team are supposedly easy and a quick fix if it's a problem. Well at least that's what I've heard from some other team members. Plus, from where I'm working I can see him sitting at his desk and it doesn't look like he is that busy.

Toya is walking back with a couple empty bins and as soon as I see her I start laughing. "Your cousin is crazy, T." "Yeah, Jazz is something else", she says. "She a different type of breed, real as ever. Don't bite her tongue for nobody and she gone tell you how she feels, whether you like it or not." "Yeah, she damn sho don't bite her tongue", I say. She already told me I was looking at your ass and everything, talking about how big it is. I told her I couldn't tell through your work outfit, I have to see you in street clothes."

"Don't worry, my butt ain't that big", she says. It just looks like that through the uniform. It's really flat as hell, just wide." "Well, I still gotta see you outside to see what you sitting on", I say. Then I can give you my opinion. Until then, I'm blind. But you can let me know when you wear only your underwear under your uniform like they say some people do so I can see if you got a jiggle." I make a little smile as I look her up and down. "I'm just saying, that's the closest way I can judge you with your uniform on. It's not like you got on some tights or some scrubs, so when you decide to rock just the Vickie sees under your uniform, let me know. I'll make sure I watch for the jiggle and then I'll let you know how it look." She started laughing, saying "boy you crazy! Ain't no way say I'm coming up in *here* like that! Yeah, you'll have to catch me outside the gate like you said." By this time we both laughing. "Well just let me know if you ever decide to do it. Won't nobody know but me and you. I know you saying no now but just think about it." She quickly interrupts. "Shit, I already thought about it, re-thought about it, answered it, and re-answered it. That ain't happening! Let me get these parts for you before I get in trouble." I watch her wide, flat ass as she walks away.

CH.2 The Inside Scoop

I managed to finish my breakfast while talking to Toya, which let me know how easy the job really is. Anytime you can manage to eat a whole meal while working it's definitely proof that the job is not hard, or at least doesn't appear to be. I guess I'll ask Larry before he get busy if he can cover me for a quick bathroom break. Plus, I don't know when the next break is, so I can't really wait until I find that out. I can see Larry standing up now, talking to another co-worker, so I motion for him to come down by me when he's done. At least I got his attention so he can't say he didn't see me. When he finally walks up, he says "what's up?" I instantly tell him that I was wondering if he could let me go to the bathroom. "I usually don't do that, and especially this close to the break", he says. I'll let you go this time *since* it's your first day but I usually don't give bathroom breaks. The bell about to ring in about fifteen minutes too, in case you didn't know." "Oh, ok", I say. "I don't think

I can wait, really." "I'll be right back though, five minutes." I can tell *that* he really doesn't want to relieve me but oh well, I have to go. It's not like I'm asking him to do the job for the rest of the day. Damn, I think I'm in the wrong area. I definitely can't work like this, not knowing if I can even get a break. Shit, *that* should be something that he *wants* to do, really. He should be giving out breaks without people asking. This whole thing and process is new to me though, so maybe *I* don't know what a team leader duties are or whatever. I thought if somebody needed something that it was their job or duty to handle the situation. I remember him saying he didn't do bathroom breaks, which is some bullshit, but he gone do some today.

    Larry finally comes and tells me to "go head". The look and vibe he is giving is definitely telling me he really does not want to let me go and I can sense it immediately. He must not know who he is dealing with. Now I have to make sure I hit him with another one later on in the day. If I'm making your day easier the least you should want to do is give out a break. Oh well, he'll be all right, I say to myself while I'm walking to the bathroom. As I'm walking back out, I hear someone calling my name. "Mase, Mase, a yo Mase." I turn and see an old high school friend that I used to hang with. "Oh shit, what up Mack? You up in here too huh?" I ask. "Hell yeah", he says. "Two years and counting. You just started?" "Yeah, man", I said. "The place that I said I was never going to work in is where I'm working in. But the bills gotta be paid and the kids gotta eat. What area you working in?" "I'm around the corner in my own little area", he says. "Ok, well I'll come back thru on the next break", I say. "I know my TL about to go crazy. He already said he don't do bathroom breaks, but fuck that, I need mines." "Oh, you got one of those", Mack says, laughing. "A lot of TL's look out for their team, but it's a few that be on some other shit, not wanting to give out breaks and shit. You'll learn the ones who look out and the ones that don't real quick." I shake my head as I walk away, thinking how easy it is to just give a break to the people on your team.

When I get back to my work area Larry is not even by my work station. I see him talking to another TL a couple of feet down from where I work. I can hear them talking about the line being down because of something on the other side. He comes down and says we should do some light sweeping if our immediate area has anything on the floor, but my area is kept pretty clean by all crews. I still use the broom to get up whatever little stuff is on the floor. You have your days where it might be a little more stuff on the floor than usual, but for the most part its kept clean. "How many times does the line go down?" I ask. "Well I guess I mean, how often does this happen?" "It depends", he says. You might get a day where everything run perfect and the line barely stop, or you can have a day where something happens and it take them hours to fix it. On a few occasions, they even let us go home because I guess they figured it would take them too long to fix the problem. This mostly happens when we launch a new vehicle model for the year and have to work out the changes and kinks on jobs. It's not that common, but you do get things that breakdown. I mean, we dealing with robots and machines so things gone break. The company act like they don't understand it, but it is what it is. Other than breakdowns, the line might stop because of jobs with ALS on them. Automatic line stopper." "What's that?" I ask. "That's where you have a job that if it isn't done by a certain point on the line so the line stops. You'll see most of them on the assembly side though. And when you stop the line too many times, the supervisor will come see you. Then you dealing with a whole different issue."

Chapter 2 The atmosphere

The bell sounds and I make sure I return the broom and dustpan to the same location that I got it from. No way I'm getting blamed for losing the broom and dustpan during my first week. I ask Larry how long is this break and he says thirteen minutes, same as last break. Now I just have to remember which way Mack said the area was in that he worked. Thirteen minutes not that long, especially when you don't know where you're going. I get to the end of the aisle and I can see him coming towards my direction. "At least you were on the right track", he says." I figured you might get thrown off, that's why I came this way. What's been up with you man? Still doing the music shit?" "*Damn*, you still remember that bullshit?" I ask. "I *been* retired from that shit. Too many politics involved." Mack starts laughing. "Well wait until you deal with the politics in here. Once you get some time in you'll see what I'm talking about." "Yeah, I remember what they were saying in orientation," I say. But I also know they probably made it seem the greatest too. They told us it's gone be some bullshit every now and then too." "Nothing like seeing it firsthand though", he says. That way you can make your own conclusion."

    Listening to Mack little speech on the plant had me anxious to see what this new chapter of my life would bring. The whole union thing was new to me, as well as this whole atmosphere. Mack told me it was a couple more people that graduated with us or around the year we graduated that worked here also. I guess it's not that bad of a place to work after all. I mean, from what I can see, more people trying to get *in* the door than *out* the door. That's something I always pay attention to when starting a new job, the amount of people that come and go. You will always have the normal complainers who always have something to say about everything, but don't realize their sixty-percent of the problem. Then you have the drama people, who usually think they know everything about the place and everybody. They the ones who mostly be the shit starters too. These people would be the same in any atmosphere, though. So, I already know they in here. If I haven't noticed anything else, I've noticed that some people are just different. They love attention and go up and beyond to get it. Whether they have a crisis going on or some type of emergency, they seek attention. They specialize in talking a lot but never really doing anything.

 I check my watch and realize I got to get back before the bell rings. "Mase, Mase", is all I hear walking back and I turn around and see Toya and Jazz walking behind me. "So how you like your job?" Toya asks. "Matter of fact, I'm gone walk you back to make sure you get there on time." Laughing, I say "oh, so you like my escort? I could use a good escort. I look at Jazz and say "you gone help her? Since ya'll working so hard but got a lot of free time." Toya bursts out laughing. "Boy, don't even play me. You know I'm working hard as a slave back there. Jazz said you should let me do the same job tomorrow if they ask you." "That's not anywhere near my call", I say. "But, I already know you want to be able to kick it with your people. You have to holler at ya boy Larry about that."

We get to my work area and Toya tells jazz she gone chill for a minute and she'll get back with her later. I can see her looking at me while she is talking, but in a staring way. Toya straight though. She kind of goofy but she far from ugly. I cannot lie about that. Whatever she telling Jazz got her looking back too, and now I'm wondering what the hell they were talking about. When Toya gets back to me I say "so ya'll talking about me?" "Why you say that?" she asks. "I'm not a genius", I say, "but it damn sure look like my name was being mentioned." "Boy, ain't nobody talking about you", she snaps back with a smile on her face. "Well at least not in a bad way. Jazz said your kind of cute and asked if you had a girlfriend and all type of bullshit. She wasn't asking for herself though, she was asking like she was going to try and hook me up or something. She crazy like that."

The whole situation got me tripping, not because of the conversation they had, but because the willingness she has to *tell* me like she not talking about herself. I guess she just cut like that or whatever. "So what you tell her?" I ask. "You were so quick to tell me how she was trying to hook you up, so what did you say? I can't even believe I'm having this discussion. This feel like some Love Jones type shit." Toya immediately starts going. "I was really just listening to her tell me about *My Life*. Since she such a relationship expert and all that. I mean. I told her I thought you were cute but it's too early to be even speaking on that because you just started. And I told her I think you got a girlfriend so I can't even look at you like that. So, you happy now? That was the whole conversation." She has this little smirk on her face with a look like she is waiting on me to say something. "I was just asking", I say. "So you have to interview me or something? You got some questions for me? Anything you want to ask, or get off your chest?" "No, I'm good", she says. "I already think I know what I need to know." "Which is nothing", I quickly say. "What you know? You can't know too much because you haven't asked anything. Unless you psychic or something, I don't know how you made your conclusion or vision you have about me." I'm trying to work and talk to her at the same time, assuming she must have her work already done. She been over here for a while and hasn't even *thought about* going to her area. "When I'm ready to ask you what I already know, I'll let you know then, how about that", she says. "Even though I think I know what I need to know already. My gut feeling be telling me stuff, and most times its right." "Hold on", I say. "You crazy. See, you think you got me all figured out? After two days, you know me huh?" At this point Toya is laughing and I guess she realized she's been over here for too long so she says she will talk with me later.

All I can do is shake my head as she walks away. She is definitely straight forward and uncut. I guess that's a good thing though. She keeps it real, or at least it seems that way.

Chapter 3 A Days Work

    I had been hearing about how people are in this automotive industry, but seeing it firsthand is definitely an experience! Larry must have noticed Toya talking to me because he walks up and says, "I see you clicked well with ole' girl you are working with. She didn't want to go back to her area." I'm still thrown off by everything so all I can say is "I guess so. She was just giving me the info on her friend and how crazy she is. A small part of me had me feeling like she was trying to hook us up." Larry is sort of laughing but sounding serious. "You gone notice in here that you have some females who wait to get preyed on and you got some who treat you like the prey. I been here for four years, came in the door married, and *still* have to explain myself to some of the same women. "Now that's crazy", I say. "Well you would think that it would slow down", he says. I just laugh it off and keep on with my day. You got some who married and you can't even tell though. So, I guess that's why some people act the way they do. I always remind myself that it's easy to get caught up in some shit up in here, but it's easier to go home." "I feel you on that", I tell him. "I'm not married yet but I definitely don't have time for no bullshit, and I'm damn sho not trying to get in any either. I already done had my share of women drama and that shit is stressful."

Lunchtime has come and I walk over to the truck to see what's om the menu. I see Mack on his way out the door so I ask him if he's going to grab some food. "Not really", he says. "I'm just making a store run. But we only got thirty minutes so I have to try to be first or second in line." "I feel you", I say. "You need every minute. Thirty minutes only twenty-five when you factor in travel time." By this time, Mack already walking through the door leaving. He determined to make that store run. I see a few more people leaving out also. I can barely remember where I parked, let alone leave out at lunchtime and make it back on time.

I'm looking over the items on the lunch truck and see she has some pizza, a few burgers, and a few other items available. The lunch menu is very different from the breakfast menu. After doing a quick scan I decide to grab a couple of slices. I don't need anything too major, just something to hold me over until I get off. I also grab a pop to try and keep me extra alert. Not like I'm sleepy or anything, I'm just trying to make sure I'm on point and paying extra attention to detail. As I'm waiting to pay, Toya and Jazz are walking up. Toya says, "you got me?" I laugh as I shake my head yes. "I might only want something out the vending machine though." "Whatever, I'm not gone break you at the truck", she says. "Plus, I might want something out the vending machine too so I have to make sure you have enough for the both of us." I look over at Jazz and she says "you started it." "You couldn't tell she was extra spoiled? All the extra shit she be doing and the way she been acting don't tell you nothing? You probably think she crazy but she just spoiled. I been dealing with this for years so I'm used to it. You'll figure it out eventually." By this time, Toya has made her way to the line. "See, I only got a slice and a juice. I know I'm worth three dollars." "I hope so", I say smiling. "If you not worth three dollars, something wrong. We can't even hang with three dollars. That's like one drink, nothing else. You definitely gone treat at least one time and it won't be three dollars." "Whatever", Toya says. "I might not ever be able to treat you because you have a girlfriend. You probably can't even come outside." "Together?", the truck lady asks, "Might as well", I say. "She gone talk trash regardless so I might as well pay for it."

We walking from the truck and I tell Toya "you swear you know me huh? You gone have to ask me something one day. You can't keep assuming everything." "I'm not assuming nothing", she says. "I already know what I need to know, I already told you that." I'm laughing with a confused look on my *face*. "You don't know shit, though" I say. "You think I have a girlfriend but you haven't asked, you just keep telling me I do. That's some bullshit but I'm gone play your little game. After today though, you can't ask me shit, so whatever you don't *think* you know you better ask me and get that shit off your chest. I'm not answering shit else. Since you got everything all figured out, I have to let you see that you don't know everything." "Really", she says. "So, if I have any questions, you not gone answer them? You just gone let me believe whatever? We haven't even officially started and you already tripping. Jazz the one keep saying she think you have a girlfriend though. She say your whole demeanor says girlfriend. That's not a bad thing in here though. You won't be around here acting thirsty like a lot of these dudes who act like they haven't ever seen a woman." "That's never been my style", I say. 'I'm more of the sit back and watch the show type of person. Never really had a problem getting a girlfriend and my last job had more women than in here, so I'm used to working around women. This shit here ain't nothing new." "I hear you", she says. "We'll see after you got some time in what you think. You probably gone be all over the place."

After laughing everything off and returning to our work areas, I can't help but think about everything that's taken place. I can already tell that working with Jazz and Toya will be very interesting. Jazz is crazy but Toya is another story. I like her style though. Straight upfront and cutting no corners. It doesn't take a brain surgeon to feel the vibe like she is digging me either. I'm gone let her play her little game and see how she really is.

I see Mack walking through so I give him the two-finger peace sign. He comes and talks with another guy before stopping by me. "I had to holler at my mans down the way", he said. "He wanted me to give something to his little side piece for lunch time but she didn't show up to the meeting spot so I had to let her know she was on some bullshit. I was rushing out this bitch and everything. Then this broad don't even show up." "Yeah, I saw you rushing up outta here", I said. "You were in a zone though. I said something, you answered, and when I looked back up you were already walking out the door." "Man", he said, "them thirty minutes ain't shit. Once you get outside you only got twenty-five minutes left, so you have to plan and strategize your moves." "I feel you on that", I say. "It's my first day though so I have to make sure I remember how the fuck to get back to my area before I go *anywhere* on lunch. I can barely remember what door I came in this morning. I ain't nowhere near ready to leave out at lunch yet." Mack quickly chimes in. "Don't worry, you'll make your way out for lunch. Eventually, you'll get you a routine and be able to fit that shit right in. I be needing that fresh air, even if it's only twenty minutes. I can't just sit in here all day and not at least peek outside. Some people don't leave out until it's time to go home, and I'm proud of them, but not me." "Hell naw", I say, laughing. I guess I got some time before I get to that level. Today was straight though, because I had this chick I started with and her cousin to talk shit to. They made the lunch go smooth. Shit, you probably know the girl cousin. She said she been here for two years, so she probably started with you or around the time you started. She said her name Jazz." Mack stats describing her and soon as he says real light-skinned, I immediately go "that's her". Mack says he used to want to holler at her but he didn't want to bullshit her and then have her run his name through the mud. He said they chit chat every now and then but keep it simple. I tell him her cousin is the same way. Mack says he has to go check on his area so he'll holler at me at the end of the day. It's like we are working but only every few minutes, and once you get the parts built up, you have some downtime. I tell Larry I'm going to grab some more parts from Toya, just in case someone comes looking for me or anything. Not like I know anyone anyway, but just in case.

I get over to Toya and she already got everything ready for me when I get there. "It's already ready boo", she says. "I figured you would be coming to get the parts so I made sure it was set up perfect. See, I be looking out. Don't forget that." All I can do is shake my head and say thanks. I don't know *what* kind of thoughts go through her mind. The bell rings as I'm walking back, and I can see Larry and Don P talking as I'm bringing the supplies back. Don P asks me how I like it so far, and tells me it will get harder as I move around, and even harder if I switch departments. He also asks me if I would like to work the rest of the week. I'm a TPT (Temporary Part-Time) worker so I am only supposed to work three days a week. I think about it for about two seconds, and say "hell yeah". I got a job to make money and have extras so I'm piling it on right now. No need to turn down money that's on the table.

The bell rings for the break which means the next bell will be the end of the day. So far, I can't complain about my new job. The workload is light and it's not too strenuous. Even if I was doing the job by myself, I still don't think that it's that hard.

More working, but I can easily deal with that. I'll take the paint shop any day over the assembly area. Don P already pretty much got me convinced on that. I don't know about in the future, but I'm definitely trying to stay in the paint shop in the meantime.

I see a few people walking around with earbuds and I'm sure they told us in orientation that it wasn't allowed. Maybe they changed the rules and the union doesn't know yet. I'll make sure I ask Larry before I leave just to get a clearer picture. Shit, if I can have some music that'll make the day go even quicker. I can *really* be in my own zone and just let the time fly by. It's like when you got the music going, everything else just seems easier. At least to me.

Since I've stocked up my work I don't have to be exactly right back when the bell rings. That's another advantage of this job. I can have my work stocked up and not have to be rushing and all that extra shit. I *have* noticed that they have a lot of women working here. More than what I imagined. I mean, I knew it was probably some women working in the automotive field, but not like this. They definitely holding down positions that hold weight. I can't see them saying that sexist shit up in here. I have to remember what my uncle told me though. Some women work their way up behind the scenes, or a different type of ladder. I guess some people do what they have to do, whether they do it the hard way or easy way. Not saying I condone the pay for play or nothing, but it's something that happens and is going to keep on happening, I'm not going to be blind and not assume some people get special treatment because of special favors. That's just the way of the world.

Mack is over at his work station so I go over there to chat with him. "Oh, you over here, huh", I say. "I had a couple extra minutes so I figured I would take a short walk in a area I haven't seen yet. Yeah, you ducked off really well." Mack just starts laughing. "Man, I love it back here. I only really see any management at the beginning of the day. After the line starts, they pretty much out of sight for the day. As long as the paint shop running good you won't see any big bosses. Assembly is different though. They always walking the floor in that motherfucker. I worked over there doing some overtime and I saw the bullshit firsthand. If it's not for overtime, guck assembly." "You sound like my supervisor", I said. "He said the same damn thing. And he a *supervisor*. That's crazy." "It just depends on where you work at", he said. "It's some easy jobs in certain areas, and it's some fucked up jobs in certain areas. That shit depends on the situation and seniority, really. Your seniority is what's the main thing in here, along with who you know. *What* you know helps, but *who* you know gets you a long way. You lucked up even getting back here, really. Usually when people start they start in assembly, but once they get rolled over to full-time they usually go to afternoons." "Yeah, that's what they said in orientation", I told him. "They also said my union steward would be the one I should speak to about that. I haven't met him yet, but they introduced themselves in orientation. Can't remember his name though." "You must be talking about Paul", Mack says. "He's the steward over here. He pretty cool though, and he doesn't take too much shit from the supervisors. He might make a few deals, but for the most part he is straight up. Slick talker, but straight up. You'll see how some stewards be friendly with the supervisors, which looks kind of crazy, but that's just how it is. I would rather see them just speak and keep it moving when it comes to management. I mean, you can have your casual conversation, but you can still be about your business." "Yeah, I feel you on that", I say. "That's like going to court and seeing the prosecutor and your lawyer having coffee together." Mack is laughing at this point and says "damn, that's a helluva way to look at it."

I've been over here for a while now so I let Mack know that I'm going back to check on my work. When I get towards my work area I see Toya and Jazz over by my station. "About time", Toya says as soon as she sees me. "See, you taking advantage of me already. You don't even know how much of your work I did while you were gone." I already know she is joking on some bullshit so I ask he how long has she been over here. "Long enough", she says. "Long enough that I loaded up your next load and you still weren't here."

"Well it sounds like you still didn't have to really do anything", I said. "I already know how much time it takes to run out of parts and it looks like I timed it right. I understand, you just wanted to come see me before we got off, huh." Toya standing there looking crazy at Jazz, with a surprised look. "Yeah, I said it", I say. "You only over here to say bye before we leave for the end of the day. But it's cool, like I said. Now I didn't have to come and find you. So we good for today." Jazz starts laughing,; "Well, I guess he told you T. He got you all quiet and shit, can't even say nothing. I can't remember when somebody had you like this, not even able to respond." "Please don't gas that boy up", Toya says. "Even though I did come over to ask you how you liked it", but never mind now. C'mon Jazz." "Aww", I say. "Let me give you a hug." I grab Toya, hug her, and whisper in her ear "you happy now", before I let her go. As I'm letting he go, she gives me a slight push away from her. "Boy, bye", she says with a smile on her face as she walks away. I can hear Jazz saying "damn, you smiling and shit" to her as they walk off. Like I said before, Toya cool. I'm just not pressed to be all on her like that.

Even though I really have a girlfriend, I'm not telling her until she asks me. She thinks she know everything so I must let her figure it all out.

I'm looking around and I'm starting to see people gathering up their things which means it's pretty much time to go. I take a look at the parts at my job and make sure it's enough for the next shift to start. I remember Larry telling me to make sure the next shift person has enough stock to start up so they won't have to come in and be rushing to get their work in order. I can respect that, because it's only the right thing to do. It wasn't a mess when I came in here today, so that's the way I want to leave it.

The bell rings and it's just as much commotion as it was at lunch time, except multiplied by ten. People are walking and talking, but doing more walking than talking. You can tell that people look forward to quitting time by the way they move. Conversations are short and to the point, and people are moving like they have a deadline. I see Toya and Jazz walking towards the door so I walk a little faster to catch up to them. Toya sees me coming so I see her tell Jazz something and Jazz walks on while Toya waits. Before I can even get over there Toya starts talking, "you about to get left". "How you leaving me and we not going to the same place?", I ask. "Maybe if we were going to the same place that could be possible, but we going to two different locations." "Whatever", she says. "I'm just trying to walk you to your car, so stop with the extra." All I can do is laugh and tell her she something else. She is beyond straight forward and doesn't hold anything back for sure. I have to remember where I parked at. All the cars damn near look the same. Toya can sense I'm looking for my car so she says, "I guess you lost now". She always has to put her opinion in, I guess. "If you weren't right here I would've found it already. I guess you throw my mind off, I just don't know if it's a good or bad thing. And there my car go right there." "Ok", she says. "But I can't throw your mind off unless you let me. I understand though. I have that effect on people." "Well who walking you to your car, since you walked me to mine?" I ask. She looks around for a quick second then says, "you lucked up today, my car right over there. Don't worry though, you walking me tomorrow and the next day after that." I stand there with a confused look on my face and she says, "yes, both days", and keeps on walking towards her car. Like I said, Toya is a different type of breed. She pretty much made it known indirectly that she has some feelings. No way she would be doing the things she's doing. She didn't have to walk me to my car. I would've eventually found it on my own. She persistent though, I can tell. And she must be super single by the way she is acting too, or on some bullshit. I want to ask her cousin but she might lie for her. Why would Jazz talk bad about her cousin? But, why wouldn't she tell me if her cousin was full of it? I'm gone ask Jazz and see what she say.

    I get am instant sense of relief as soon as I sit down in my car. It's not that I'm just that tired, but I guess it's just the fact of being on your feet all day and it taking it a toll on your body. That was the main thing people kept telling me, "if you can get past the standing, you'll be fine." They ain't *never* lied. It definitely feels like I haven't sat down all day. Now I have to get my mind right for this thirty minute drive home. On a weekend or a day where most people don't have to work, the freeway would be somewhat empty. During the week and rush hour though, traffic can be very stressful. It would normally take about twenty minutes for me to go across town, but I already know that I'm about to be driving for at least thirty minutes. That's the only downfall with this job so far. The travel. If the pay wasn't what it was then I would feel like I'm wasting a lot of gas money, but it takes a little off the edge because I don't feel like I'm just breaking even. As I'm driving, I can't help but to think about how crazy Toya is. Incredible attitude, but real as ever. Only time will tell where this goes.

    I can see the freeway entrance coming up and just like I thought, the traffic is backed up entering the freeway. I thought about taking the street but the lights would really make the trip ridiculous. After I get some time in maybe I'll move a little closer, but I like living outside the city. Peaceful and quiet is a must with me. I grew up around the stuff off the news so now I have to progress, not regress. I used the GPS just to see exactly how long it would take me, and just like I thought, it took twenty-seven minutes. I pull up in my carport like "damn, about time."

Most people think I stay far but it's only far if you live in the city. Or on the other side of the city in another suburb. Southgate is quiet and everyone pretty much keeps to themselves and goes about their business. Perfect area for me. I love the atmosphere and the fact that everything is right close by. I've been here for about a year on my own, and have about two months before my girlfriend comes to live with me. Yes, Toya is right, I do have a girlfriend, but until she asks me, I'm not volunteering any information.

I'm really hoping I can somehow stay on the day shift instead of being bumped to the night shift. I like working mornings and would definitely prefer that so I can have my evenings and weekends to myself. I can deal with getting up early to have Friday, Saturday, and Sunday off. Saturday and Sunday are not even required on a regular so I will be able to go out of town or whatever and not miss any days. I got a while to think about all that. First I have to make sure I keep my attendance and work performance up to par so I can get a full-time position. I remember from orientation that you have to be employed full-time to maximize all the benefits and perks, such as bonuses, vacations, and paid time off. No need to half step and leave money on the table. I have to max out my time here, however long that may be.

Rushing home, I forgot somehow to grab something to eat so I guess I will call in some Chinese food for dinner. I really don't feel like cooking anything, especially now, so Chinese it is. I'm mad at myself for not thinking about this before I got all relaxed and shit. The plus is that I don't have to worry about lunch tomorrow because I will have leftovers. Never have I ate all my Chinese food at one time.

When I get back in the car and hit the main street, I do a quick glance at the many options for food and entertainment. I really don't have to go to the city for any shopping or anything. Only to see family and friends. I have everything around me in close driving distance. A mall ten minutes away, and whatever type of food I prefer or groceries even closer. I can deal with the traffic for work, that's nothing really.

I get up to the restaurant and notice it's a few more cars than usual. I guess more people were thinking take out like me. Not too many people can make Chinese food at home anyways. I've definitely never had sesame chicken at *any* event gathering, holiday meal, or nothing. The lady at the counter recognizes me when I get to the counter and takes the egg roll out the bag. Yes, I'm kind of picky when it comes to food. Well not picky, I just eat certain things and don't eat other things. I can already tell by the way my food smells that the shrimp is well steamed and cooked. It's a certain kind of smell that I notice when I open the box that lets me know my food is fresh. Yeah, some people call it cats and dogs, well my spot got some of the best cats and dogs around. People stay pulling up.

I might as well set my alarm now just in case I get caught up in my night and fall asleep. I I have to make sure to leave a little bit earlier just in case the traffic is crazy. Morning traffic is so unpredictable. I then text my girlfriend Sarah to see how she is doing and if she is coming over. Sarah is pretty cool. Laid back like me and real down to earth. We've been together about two years now and I don't see it ending anytime soon. She gets along with my daughter so that's a major plus for me. We live about fifteen minutes from each other, without having to get on any freeways or anything, so that's perfect. I'm sure things will be a little different when she moves in but it won't be my first time living with someone. People have habits and that's all I want to see, her habits. I can deal with everything else. I already know how she is, but not on a full-time level. She does cook and keep her own place up to par so I know she good in those areas. It's a big step and a life changer, but it's something that has to be done to make sure we're *compatible* and not *combatible* with each other. Only time will tell.

Sarah says she will be over in about an hour so I get all my nighttime duties out the way just in case she needs the bathroom. I didn't ask her if she ate already or not but I brought her some food anyways. It'll be a little surprise for her just in case she is hungry. If not, then she already has her lunch for tomorrow. Either way, she doesn't have to worry about food. I try to be equal fair in a relationship. Give her a break every now and then from the kitchen. I guess I'll take me a shot of the vodka I got in the freezer to help me wind down my night. I don't have to worry about hearing the door or anything because she can let herself in, so I can relax in the room until she gets here.

    I'm kind of looking forward to my next day at work. I wonder will I be doing the same job that I did today, or will I be doing something different. The job today was only a portion of how a regular day would be, so that job as a whole wouldn't be shit. If I even get to do that job. they might switch me on to something else to see how I work in a different area. The good thing about it is Don P already told me to report to the same area for the week so maybe that means I'm doing the same thing. I hope so, if not, oh well, the money still adding up. I just hope traffic be a little lighter than today. Really don't feel like dealing with the stop and go.

When Sarah gets in, the first thing she says is "hey baby". This has been a ritual of hers for years that's been going on forever. Of course, she is shocked that I picked up the food already, but glad that I did because she hadn't eaten yet. We chit chat about our days and call it a night.

Chapter2: Day 2

The next morning starts off on a good note. The traffic is definitely lighter than usual. Those ten extra minutes made a big difference and even gave me time to hit McDonald's. I can get used to leaving earlier to deal with a damn near empty freeway. Less cars, and less fools rushing and tearing shit up.

When I pull into the parking lot I can see the difference already. Parking spaces are pick and choose. No quick shuffling and fast walking needed. Smooth process. I just hope my badge works because we were told some new employees have been having a hard time with their badge at the gate. I swipe my badge across the scanner and boom, the light turns green. Now I can be situated and ready when the line starts.

While I'm walking towards my work area, I can hear someone slightly yell "hey boo". I can tell by the voice who it is, and when I turn around of course it's Toya. I tell her good morning and she comes right back with "that's it"? "All you gone say is good morning"? by this time we're walking side by side and I ask "so what else you want"? "You could've gave me a hug too", she says. "Maybe that would start my day off on a good note." I don't even know how to take in all this now. It's too early. "Ok", I say to her. "Today I'm boo and you want a hug. I guess you didn't get a hug before you left this morning. No kiss on the cheek or nothing?" now she looking at me side-eyed with a smirk on her face. "A hug or kiss from who?" she says. "I don't have no one to do all that with so just give me my damn hug". I'm laughing as I give her a hug. "Did that kill you?" she asks. "That's all I wanted, a hug. You lucky I didn't kiss you." "Really", I say. "You feeling it this morning I see. You got your demands and all. You acting like your name hold weight or something. I'll let you call the shots this morning." Jazz is walking up at this time and she doesn't make anything better. "Damn, yall rode together this morning? That's what's up." "C'mon now Jazz, you tripping", I say. "You know damn well we didn't ride together. Toya definitely not ready for no shit like that." Jazz quickly respond. "Well you could have picked her up this morning, I don't know." "Well", I say, "the day you hear about us riding here together means we left from the same place." Jazz can't do anything but laugh. Toya is just shaking her head. "I want my breakfast too, so I'll meet you at the truck when the bell rings." I don't even answer and Jazz is walking off with her yelling "see you when the bell ring." "Yall crazy", I say, as they walk off.

    Larry must have came in around the same time as me because when I go over to his desk, he is already sitting, waiting on the bell. Computer on and all. He definitely didn't just walk in at the last minute, like he did yesterday. I guess he ready to do some work, or at least he appears ready. I might give him a break on the bathroom run today, but if I have to go, I have to go. It won't kill him to do some work for a couple of minutes. Maybe he stuck in his ways or whatever, but I could care less about all that.

I think I'll start my work early to get a jump on things. That will give me more downtime and maybe make the day go smoother. I been noticing a few people walking around with headphones on today too. I know what they told us in orientation, but these rules apparently get bent once you hit the floor. It seems like it's up to the people discretion. If no one says anything, fine. If they do, then they take them off, I guess. That seems like the attitude of most people, but I don't think I'm ready to test them waters yet. I'm too fresh on the scene.

The bell has rung but the line hasn't started yet. Larry is now walking around looking as if he is looking for someone. I hear a couple people saying they need someone for something, but I can't make out what they're saying. Oh well, I can't really help the situation so I take a load back while they fix whatever problem is going on. I can take advantage of all this and *really* get ahead on my work.

Toya is sitting at a table in her work area when I get back there. It doesn't look like their working back here either. Toya sees me walking towards her and yells "hey boo", which causes a couple people to turn their heads in our direction. "I see it's slow back here too", I say. "Shit, I guess so", she says. "I don't know, I guess some people absent or something. I heard some people saying something but I'm just taking advantage of the situation. Jazz told me we might have some mornings like this." "Yeah, I feel you", I say. "I guess I should be sitting down on my ass too somewhere. I'll holler at you later." I drop off the parts and make my way back to my area. I can hear her say "don't forget my breakfast" as I'm walking off.

Larry is working on a job when I return to the work area. I ask him what's going on and he says a few people called in so he has to be on a job unless they find someone to send him. I'm thinking, how the hell they about to just find someone when they don't even have an option at this point? "So how you just gone find somebody out the blue?" I ask. "Usually when something like this happen, they canvass around the plant to see if people have extra people", he said. "After that, they see who can use whoever in different areas and send people to those areas." "Oh, ok", I say. "I figured they wouldn't let you stay on a job all day, seeing that they need you off the line." "That shit don't matter", he says. "Ii been on a job for the whole day before, so it wouldn't surprise me. They care about the TL being off the line, but if the TL has to be on the line, then that's what it will be. I don't really worry about it though. If they send somebody, fine, if not, I'm right here. I get paid by the hour and not the unit. That's the supervisor's problem."

After loading up a few more parts, I check my phone to see what time it is. The first break is coming up. Time is moving kind of fast today it seems. I hope the whole day goes like this. Just as I'm finishing up, the bell rings. I guess I will be nice and buy this girl breakfast. When I get over to the truck, the line is long as hell. Maybe they serving some different shit, or people didn't get up early enough to stop or whatever, but this shit ridiculous today. Hopefully they won't snatch up all the good shit. I see Mack walking towards the truck and we give each other a "what's up" nod. I should've told him to grab a French toast breakfast since he will be there before me. I'm damn near there though, I just hope they don't sell out.

I do a quick glance when I get to the truck to see if they still have French toast and just like I figured, that shit gone. Oh well, she'll be eating pancakes today. I also grab a couple of orange juices. By the time I'm done paying, Toya and Jazz are walking towards the truck. "I told you I had breakfast coming", Toya tells Jazz. "So yall had a bet or something?" I ask Toya. "No, but I told Jazz you were getting me breakfast. That was it." "But you didn't know if I had it yet, did you?" I asked. "I knew you were going to buy it so that's why I told Jazz that", she said. She said it with so much confidence that I couldn't even reply. I gave her the pancakes and orange juice and she instantly started smiling. "You got the orange juice too? That's what's up." I can tell that she outdone by the orange juice. "Well I figured you would need something to drink so I got the juice", I said. At this point, her and Jazz are walking away. She looks back and says, "thanks boo", and I can feel people looking to see who is she is speaking to. Even Mack has a confused look on his face. He instantly says, "she on your head". I laugh it off saying, "I don't know *what* she on, really. She a different type of breed. I can sense that she is sending signals though, she is making that known." "I can see that, too," Mack says. "I don't even be around like that, but the few times I have, I can tell. Plus, she wouldn't be acting like that in front of people. She could've just got the food from you without saying anything. She didn't have to say shit, especially after she had already walked away." "That was the same thing I was thinking", I said. "I'm like, damn, you could've said thanks when I first gave it to you. I already knew it was an audience, she put the spotlight on it though. It is what it is. People always make their own conclusion anyway, even if they don't know the situation." Mack agrees. "You already know that! People who don't even know you will make all kinds of assumptions just by seeing you walking with someone or talking with someone. You will realize how nosy people really are. Most people don't give a damn about what the next person does, but you have your few news reporters that keep everybody else name in their mouth. And it's not just the women. A lot of these dudes be just as nosy as the women in here." I just shake my head. "Hell naw. I guess I have to make sure I don't give them nothing to talk about."

Larry is training this guy on the job as I'm walking up. I guess he finally found someone to do the job. I give the guy a nod as I walk by to my area. Larry said the guy's name but I didn't catch it. I'll do my own introduction when I'm ready. I'm friendly, but I'm not a talk show host. You will get limited words out of me unless I've known you for a while. Hell, even then the words might be limited. I'm trying to get my work done so I can eat my breakfast. When I get to my area, I realize I already have a load of parts done, ready to go. I guess I was working faster than I realized. Maybe I will get another load done to really have some downtime. Larry comes up and starts telling me how they had to bring the guy from the assembly side. It doesn't make any difference to me anyway, but I just listen. I do kind of want to check out the assembly side just to see what's it's like, even though people be bashing it. "So, it may come a time when I have to go to assembly?" I ask Larry. "I can't guarantee anything", he says, "but they usually have more people than they need. They rarely need anyone from assembly, only in desperate situations. Today was just one of those days that you get once in a while. It *has* been a few occasions where some people were sent from paint to assembly, but that was due to weather. It was too many call-ins and they didn't have enough people on standby so they asked us to send some people to fill in for the day. But, that's very rare. That's like the last resort."

By the time Larry is done talking, I'm pretty much done with my load of parts. I have to ask him about the job I'm doing, and when the person who is assigned to the job will be back. I don't want to be moved around the plant every day and be doing something different every day. The situation he was speaking on was different, but I just want to get some information regarding my own life. I know I just started, but if I can get in an area and be there every day, then that's the route I'm trying to take.

I have two bins full now so I can take these back and have some extra downtime. When I get back there, I see Toya running a machine, with headphones on! Not the big headphones but the small earbuds. She sees m and takes one out of her ear. "Hey boo, you working hard?" "Not really", I say. I guess she not going to stop with the boo stuff. "How was breakfast?" I ask. "That shit hit the spot", she says. "I might not even have to eat lunch, thanks to you." Feeling like she just talking shit I say, "now you know you were going to eat regardless. Don't make it seem like you wouldn't have eaten if I didn't get the food." She is laughing as she says "what if I left my money at home? You don't even know my story." Sensing bullshit I say "your story, what story? You act like you have a major issue or something. That's that dramatic bullshit. You know you got money to buy whatever and you would've spent it if I didn't get your food. So, stop tripping and fix your face. You got your way."

    I walk away as Toya has a small smirk on her face. I'm going to try and get as far ahead as I can so maybe I can get a few extra minutes for lunch. Even if I get done five minutes before, that will give me time to use the bathroom and get a head start. Every minute counts. Before I go to my area, I walk around and see if I see

Mack. I'm not used to the place yet, so a lot of things look the same. I have to find a landmark or something to let me know I'm in the right area. I see Jazz talking to another young lady so I go over and ask her if she knows Mack. She can't "picture him", neither can the girl she is talking to. I hear someone yelling "yo" in the background and turn and see Mack standing in a small back corner.

"Dude, they got you ducked off from damn near everybody", I say. "That's the best part", he says. "They don't have to come looking for me or be wondering where I'm at because it's no reason to even be back here. If management come back here it's because they really have to. I get my own parts, so I don't have to wait on nobody to bring me anything. How can I complain about that? I'm good." "I see", I say. I can hear some music playing from a small speaker so I ask him if anyone has said anything about it. "Not yet", he says. "If they say something I'll just turn it off, but until then, I'm bumping it. It's not like I have it real loud or anything, I just keep it at a level I can hear and do my job." I tell him how I noticed a few people with the earbuds in their ears and he tells me that they really haven't been tripping about them lately. As long as no one gets hurt or messes up anything, management probably won't enforce it. I can't understand it anyway. No headphones will ever be louder than the machines. "Just try to be discreet when you are walking around", he says. "I *have* seen a few people get warnings because of the earbuds, though. The hi-lo drivers and tugger drivers be working through break sometimes, so they might trip if they see you wearing them then too. Just try to be discreet with them and you should be ok." "Ok", I say. "I see you be dipping out every day at lunch. You leave out every day?" "Damn near", he says. I just be needing some fresh air. Get a little environmental refresher." "I think I'm going out today", I say. "I might get me a little routine to have at lunch. Maybe the days will go a little faster."

    I head back to my area and Larry is assisting the other guy on the job. I guess the guy hasn't grasped the job yet. Larry sees me coming and doesn't say anything but just shakes his head. His silent language is saying "unbelievable". I walk right past and give a little smirk of my own while shaking my head. I guess this is one of the moments that Larry talked about. Some people get the job right away and sometimes it takes a little longer. The job doesn't look that hard but everyone is different. Different mind state, different mentality, and different ambition. Nobody is the same. I've only been here a couple days and I already can tell that every job isn't meant for everybody. Height can be a problem for some people as well. It just depends on the job. You just have to find something that fits you.

It's almost time for lunch so I start moving a little faster to make sure I get ahead of schedule. Even if I don't roll out with Mack I still will be able to hit the store myself. I just know I'm not staying in this building today.

As I'm working, I see Don P from a distance and he is walking around talking with everyone. He seems pretty cool. Not too stern and not hovering over you, watching you all day. That shit is unnecessary and un-called for. More like intimidation in my opinion. It doesn't take all the extra shit to be a good supervisor. I catch eye contact with him before he gets up to me and give a "what's up" nod. He asks if I'm good and do I like the job. he also tells me that I might go to assembly after I go full-time. He doesn't know for sure, but he tells me it's something he heard through the grapevine but not etched in stone. He also says Paul (Union Steward) should have the information if it's official. I don't really care where I'm at, if I'm on the payroll. I can learn anything with the right raining. If I get moved to assembly then oh well, assembly it is. Hopefully I can get the same hours and stay on days, but I'll cross that bridge when the time comes.

I'm finishing up a load to take over to Toya when I hear someone say, "I love a man that works." By the time I sit the box down to see who it is, Toya is right there. "What's up T?" I say. "I guess you ahead in your work." "You already know", she says. "I'm trying to see what you doing for lunch. I'm not really hungry though, I'm just seeing what you are doing." I don't know where she is going with this, but I'm going to hear her out. "Well I might ride out with my mans Mack, but I don't know. I'm still trying to decide. I'm not staying in for lunch though. I have to get some fresh air." She immediately invites herself. "I need some fresh air too. Where we going?" I can't believe she just invited herself, really. "So you just gone invite yourself huh?" I ask. "I'm pretty sure you were going to ask me", she said. "I'm just answering your question in advance. You'll rather have me in your passenger seat anyway." "You swear you know me", I say. "I just go along with it but you really don't know me. You got some parts right and some parts twisted. But I guess you can ride with me t lunch. Have your ass by the door so we can walk straight out." "I'm already on my way out there", she says. "I made sure to work ahead so I can leave early from my work station."

She walks off and I do a quick survey of my area to make sure everything is set up for when I get back. I don't want to have to be rushing to get back to work. I like to be organized and have things go smooth.

When I get over by the door I can see Toya talking with some guy so I just keep walking and go straight out the door. I'm not the type to interrupt you if you are talking, especially if you're not my girl. I stay in my own lane.

I get a few steps outside the door and hear Toya. "So you was just gone leave me? It's like that?" "Look", I tell her, "I'm not a Secretary of State type of dude. I'm not pulling a number. You knew I was coming that way so you should've been ready. I'm not going to interrupt you if you are talking. That's not my style. Once I saw you and dude talking I was like oh, okay, and kept it moving. I don't want to look like a hater. I don't know *what* you and he were talking about." "He was just chit-chatting", she said. "You know, doing his little introduction or whatever." "Well I'm glad I didn't interrupt", I said. "He was trying to get his game on and I would've killed the whole mood." She quickly tries to shut down anything. "Whatever, he wasn't talking about nothing really, anyway."

Luckily, I remembered where I had parked my car, so getting out the lot was pretty easy. I saw Mack on the way to my car. He gave me a nod and said he waited a couple of minutes but didn't see me. "I'm on another move anyway", I say as Toya walks up right after me to my car. "I see", Mack says as he keeps walking to his car. Traffic should be clear around this time. I'm only going to the store anyway so it shouldn't be a problem. Toya says to grab her some snacks, nothing in particular, so I get her some Doritos and a Reese's. I get myself a Kit Kat and a juice. I hop in and hand her the bag. She takes out the Kit Kat and I let her know that's mines. After hearing her spoiled ass go on about why I didn't get her a Kit Kat, I tell her she can have it. I also remind her that she didn't make any requests before I went in the store, and let her know that she lucky to even be riding with me because I don't know her like that. She smirks and says "whatever".

    I check my phone for the time and see that it only took sixteen minutes for the store run. I can deal with that. As long as I get out within the first five minutes, I'm good. Toya says thank you for letting her go to the store. It really wasn't a big deal to me letting her go. My day didn't change one bit. We walk in together and go our separate ways towards each other's work areas. The time is moving at a good pace. Half the day is over and I hope the second half goes as fast.

Larry is sitting with his head down when I walk up towards my area. I guess he tired from doing the little bit of work he had to do. It's not like he was doing some strenuous shit or nothing, I guess he just not used to it. That's crazy. Take a job but don't really want to actually do the job.

I guess I will do another load before I take the other two back to Toya. I'm ahead of schedule so I don't have to rush or anything. That's an advantage of doing this job. Whoever got this job on a regular has it gravy. You work at your own pace and once you get ahead, you should be ahead all day. How could you not love that? I'm going to dread the last day doing this shit.

When I get over to Toya, she is sitting with her back to me, talking to Jazz. As I get closer, I can hear Jazz talking, along with a male's voice. When I finally get over there, I can see that they are talking to the same guy that was talking to Toya before lunch. I don't want to make it seem like nothing so I give a quick "what's up" nod to everyone. Jazz says, "what's up Mase" in a surprising tone like she is shocked that I'm not sticking around. "Nothing much", I say. "Just dropping off the parts so I can have me some extra downtime. I see ya'll back here chilling." "If that's what you call it", Toya says. "That's what you doing", I say, with emphasis. "Well I'm about to hit the vending machine while I got time." I turn to walk back towards the vending machine and I can feel like Toya wanted to say something but she didn't. Oh well, when you busy sometimes you miss out.

Jazz pulls up on me while I'm at the vending machine. "Toya said grab her some chips." I quickly shoot that down. "No, she didn't. She barely said anything while I was right there, so I know she didn't ask you to tell me after I left. Plus, she can have dude get her some chips. Shit, that's her company, right? Ok then. Tell her to tell dude she want some chips. I am NOT the flunky guy." "Why you gotta be like that?" Jazz says laughing. "So you not buying her chips because she was talking to that guy? That's some bullshit." I quickly respond. "No, her sending the message through *you* is the bullshit.

That's the same dude she was talking to before lunch by the door. But you weren't around for that episode." Jazz starts laughing. "Well I can't speak on that but I'm talking about right now. I guess that's between you and her. That's Tom. He works over there by Toya. We started at the same time. "Well I really don't give a damn *what* his name is. He better do all her gopher shit then, because I'm not the one. If she going to be running off at the mouth with him, she might as well put him to work." Jazz can't stop laughing. "You crazy", she says. "I understand where you are coming from though. I'll probably react the same way. Shit, don't be all up in somebody else face and then ask me for something. Fuck that. I'll be like ask that bitch to buy it. Yeah, the more I think about it, that is some bullshit." "Ok then", I say. "So tell her that when you go back over there." "Well he started talking to her when you started coming back there, it seems like", Jazz says. I guess I opened up his eyes to something new and now he trying to put his bid in.

    I head back to my work area thinking like I'm glad to have a girlfriend because these chicks too friendly nowadays. They talk and laugh with everybody. Hell, my girl might be friendly too, for all I know. I don't put shit past nobody. I'm not gone sit and worry myself to death either, but I know how sneaky women can be.

Larry is sitting at his desk when I walk back up. I guess the guy he was training finally got the hang of it. Halfway through the day but at least he got it. I bet Larry damn near ready to go to sleep now. He ate two breakfast meals this morning, had to work, ate again at lunchtime, and had to work *after* lunch? Yeah, he definitely tired. He probably damn near ready to leave right now. It's really not any hard jobs in this area, but like they say, everybody different.

After looking over my work, I decide to finish up a few more bins of parts so I can have damn near a hour of downtime. I won't have to take anything back to Toya because she will be stocked up and she won't have to come get any parts because she will have enough to work with. Plus, it will give her a break from me. I don't want to seem like I'm trying to block dude game or anything either.

The bell rings just as I'm finishing up another bin, so I decide to just chill out in my work area on the break. It's a makeshift chair made out of some empty containers so I grab one and pop a squat. As I'm playing a game on my phone I get a tap on my shoulder. I look back and see Toya. "So, you weren't going to come and see me?", she asks. "Well it looked like you already had company", I said. "You already know I'm not interrupting shit if you already got something going on, so I just left. Waiting around isn't my style." "He was just talking to me damn", she says. "Asking me where I used to work and do I like my job so far. Nothing really." "I didn't ask what he said, I was just telling you why I didn't hang around", I said. "It wasn't a reason for me to be hanging around. You were pre-occupied." "Mason, you tripping", Toya says. "I really can't stop somebody from coming over here. And he really just came over here for the first time today. I guess he saw you come back here and was trying to see who you were." "And what you tell him?" I ask. "Nothing", she says. "What was I supposed to tell him, you were my boyfriend or something? He said he saw us leave out at lunch too. I was like damn, you watching me or something." "Hell naw", I say. "You got a stalker already and barely been here a week.

He probably wondering where you at right now." "I hope not", she says. "He doesn't even know me like that to be looking for me. You just make sure you don't leave without seeing me." "If you got a chaperone, I'm leaving", I say.

After Toya leaves, Larry comes up and says, "I see you made you a friend, or did you know her already?" "I just met her when I started here", I say. "I guess she just like talking to me. Nothing spectacular though. Just passing the time." "That's what you call it, huh", Larry says. "Well, we gone roll with that for today and I'm gone ask you the same thing in a couple weeks. You might have a different answer by then." I laugh as he walks off. I'm not really thinking about Toya like that. I got enough going on already without adding some extra bullshit on top of it.

The line stops running for a few minutes but I keep working to give myself some extra time once it starts back up. I figure if I do about two more loads I won't have to do anything else today. Pretty sure that'll be enough to last until the end of the day. I can take two loads back to Toya and that will definitely be enough to last on her end.

When I get back there, Tom is standing by her talking, watching her work. Damn, he could at least help her if he just gone stand there. She doesn't even see how the shit looks, but that's for her to figure out. I can't tell her how to get people in order and set standards. If she lets him stand there while she works and not say anything, then that's on her. He on some bullshit too because he could offer to help, since he is making her get behind in her work. At least make her day easier. If she hasn't been taught a certain way, it's too late now. I drop off the parts and give them both a nod. Toya is definitely a friendly ass female.

When I get back to my work area I can see that the line is still down. Hell yeah! Exactly what I needed. Chill time at the end of the day. It doesn't look like the line is starting anytime soon either because a lot of people sitting down or walking around. A few people are sweeping, but most are doing their own thing. We have about an hour before it's time to leave and I'm already three bins ahead. One more will give the next shift more than enough to start up with.

Larry comes up and tells me we're probably finish for the day and will leave about thirty minutes early. I don't care if it's only ten minutes, anything early is good. I finished my last bin and took a seat by my work station to wait until they tell us we can leave.

From where I'm sitting I can see the immediate area around me, as well as a few aisles over. I see Toya walking towards me but she doesn't see me until she gets closer. She sees me with my jacket on and says "oh, you already knew we were leaving early". "I was on my way over here to tell you but you already ready. Plus I came over here to give you this." She leaves a folded-up piece of paper on my computer, and when she walks off I open it to find her number written down. Slick way to do it but I'm not surprised. I already knew she had some slick ways and this proved it. Maybe she trying to be lowkey, but that shit went out the window a long time ago. Even Larry sees how she is acting. Nothing major to me, but people turn nothing into something real quick.

Speaking of Larry, he comes up with his jacket on and says "well, five minutes to go. I guess we can start heading for the gate." I don't even respond at first, I just grab my backpack and put my jacket on. Then I think about it." Yo, Larry, if we leave early do we get paid for the rest of the day?" "Well not the TPT's", he says. "Your time stops when the clock stops. Everybody else still get paid for the rest of the day. They call it short work week. So no matter if we leave at eight in the morning or right after lunch, we still get paid." "That shit should apply for everybody", I say. Who thought of that shit?" "Well you have to ask your steward about that", he says. "He can get into detail about all that type of stuff." "Will do", I say as I walk towards the door.

I text Sarah once I get in my car to see how her day is going at the bank. She is a banking specialist at a major bank and I'm pretty sure she has some stressful days dealing with the public. I also want to see if she's coming over after work and if she s cooking today. No matter what, I still think when it's all said and done I will end up with Sarah. She understands me as a whole and gets me, without me having to explain every little thing. I also put Toya's number in my pocket for a rainy day. More like a thunderstorm day. I'm not in a rush to start a headache.

From the looks of it, I guess the early exit helped in a major way. The freeway isn't as bad as it usually is and the traffic is moving smoother than usual. If only we got off at this time every day. That's another wish, though. In the meantime, I'll enjoy this because I don't know when the next one will be.

When I get home, I take some steaks out to cook so when Sarah gets here she won't have to handle the cooking. I've stayed on my own before so I learned how to make a few meals. She still will be surprised because she thinks I'm going to wait on her. I'll get all my night time duties out of the way too so she can have the bathroom to herself. Maybe I'll hit up Toya with a random text message. Never mind that, I'll just holler at her tomorrow. She won't be looking at me like some thirsty dude.

Sarah comes in while I'm relaxing on the couch and says, "what you get?" She hasn't looked in the kitchen yet but can smell the aroma. "I got in the kitchen", I tell her. "I knew you would think I brought something. I made it when I came in from work. So now we have something like Outback for dinner. "Ummhmm", she says. "It smells good though. Right on time." Another easy, peaceful night. Never can have too many of these.

Chapter: So Far So Good

It's been a few weeks since I started this new chapter in my life, and I must say that so far, I can't complain. I'm making more than I've ever made at any job, I'm still on dayshift, we get raises every year, and I get excellent job benefits. I mean, what else can you want from a company? Not too many places are going to give pay raises every year, while having free insurance. That's rare as hell. I can deal with the work. That definitely isn't a issue. The atmosphere isn't really a problem either. I know what I'm there to do and that's the main goal for me. Get my money and stay away from bullshit.

You get a certain routine for things after you do them on a regular basis, and that applies to adapting to a new environment as well. You also learn a few more ways to maneuver and handle situations. I had already known the area from general knowledge and moving around, but I still made sure to learn it a little bit better to make things less stressful. Restaurants, shopping, convenience stores; I made sure I knew all the shortcuts and quickest ways to get where I needed to be. Definitely can't be trying to get directions on my lunch break.

Toya has been very social since she gave me her number, even though I still haven't used it. I guess she uses the time at work to talk about whatever she would if we spoke outside of work. I have to admit, she does help keep the time going. Maybe I'll surprise her and buy her lunch today. I don't know, though. Her little buddy might ruin it for her.

Things are still pretty cool at the job, and I even was offered a full-time position that I declined. Yes, I had to. I never decide the first time if I don't have to. I always have to weigh my options. That's the way I live. I told the employment people that I have to think about it, and that I will let them know by the end of the day.

My heart is in the medical field but my situation won't allow me to just wait on a call that may never come. I guess my decision has been made. Auto industry it is!

I felt a certain type of feeling when I walked into work the next day. The feeling of excitement, satisfaction, and a sense of calm comes over me instantly. Of course, Sarah was extra excited when I told her that I was going to be full-time. She had been asking for the past couple of days so I know she is relieved too. I've been trying to secure a financial foundation for my family and now I have the opportunity to do so.

I see Larry when I get over by the work area and inform him that I accepted the position for full-time. He reiterates that I might be going to another shift now that I'm full-time. That's the bullshit but I didn't want to take too long deciding on whether I wanted to be full-time or not. Don P already had told me that it wasn't a guarantee that I would be bumped to another shift, so I'm trying not to worry about it. If it happens, it happens.

I'm setting up my work station when Toya walks up. "Good morning boo", she says. "I guess the only time I'll have to talk to you is at work, huh. This the longest I ever had to wait on a call. But I remember, you got a girl so I know your time is limited." "You swear you know", I say laughing. "I might just be seeing where your head at. Seeing how you gone act up in here. Plus, I'm sure you don't be bored after work. Hell, you not bored *at* work. Your little fan club keep you busy. I'm probably not the only one with the number either." "Why you think that?" She asks. She can barely keep the smile off her face when she is talking. "See, I say. The look on your face answering my question. Pretty sure you got some fans in here." "You don't know *what* I got", she snaps back laughing. "You just assuming. I'm just little ole' T. Don't nobody know me like that in here." "I hear you" I say. "Only time will tell."

After the day gets started, I see Larry talking to Don P and then I see Don P heading my way. "So, you already know a couple things might change now that you switching to full-time. I can try and put a word in but you know, that's hit or miss. So be prepared for the worst, that's all I can tell you." He told me to also remember that it's a few people that's out on medical, so they might not be returning for months. That could keep some spots open on days and maybe give me a chance to stay on days. I have to burn it out as long as I can. Hopefully something will happen where it works out permanently and I remain on first shift. At least I know how my days will go, instead of wondering what job I will be on and floating around the plant.

As I'm dropping off a load to Toya, I'm looking around the atmosphere and noticing that it's a lot of females that work in here. I also notice that it's a guy in damn near every one of their faces. All I can do is laugh to myself. I see the women working and the guys standing there, talking. Shit crazy! I get the women wanting and loving all the attention, but they not even making it hard for the dudes. The dudes talking and the women working. The women don't see it like it's wrong though. I guess that's the thing in here.

Tom is at the vending machine when I get over by Toya and I give him a little "what's up" nod. He seems ok as far as I can see but

I really don't fuck with new people. Nothing meant by it but that's just me. I keep to myself and deal with those that I've been dealing with. I grab me a Reese's and Toya some chips and keep it moving. Don't want to hear her mouth about why I didn't get her nothing. She can damn near see the vending machine from her area so I'm glad she didn't see me. She'll be surprised.

    When I finally get back there, Tom is back there, sitting and talking with Toya. Looks like Toya has her some snacks too, already. I guess that's why Tom was at the vending machine, copping her shit. Good, I'm keeping my Reese's. I don't even want it, but she damn sure not getting it now. I hit her with a "what's up T" as I sit the parts down. She has this confused look on her face like she surprised at my actions. No need to be, really. I guess she thought I was going to hang around or whatever. Whatever she does is what she does. I'm not trying to stop it and I can't stop it anyway. That's all on her to deal with. I just won't be a part of whatever game she is playing. I guess Tom has one of them extra easy jobs where he can chill and walk around whenever he feels like it. Mack told me to try and work my way through the system and let the system work for me. I guess that's what Tom did.

Damn I hope I get to stay on dayshift. My life is perfect for first shift. I already have everything in the order and on the days I like and prefer. I won't let it strain my brain though. I have to knock these parts out so I can get ahead on my work. I might try and catch Mack and ride out with him at lunch. Hit the store up or something. I haven't even been checking up on the time while I'm thinking about lunch. Damn, at this point I don't even have time to look for Mack. If I see him, then it's cool, if not, that's cool too. I just know I can't waste minutes.

When I get outside I don't see Mack anywhere around when I do a quick glance so I keep it moving to my ride. I hope the food spot in the gas station not crowded. I definitely have to put something in my stomach before I start to get a headache. I see a few other people that work in my area too. I guess this where some people come if they want a quick meal other than the regular fast food. It's still the same pretty much, plus it's done already so the wait isn't long. The line is moving quick too at the register, so I only spent six minutes for the whole process. I even got time to eat a little bit when I get back before the line start. Not to mention that I'm already ahead in my work from earlier. The afternoon should go by fast.

    I see Jazz while I'm walking back in the building and the first thing she says is "damn, you eating good. You could have told somebody you were getting something different. I would've paid for my own shit." "It wasn't even like that, really", I tell her. "I decided this at the last minute and was like fuck it, I'm going out for lunch." "I bet", she says. "So Toya got something too? She better not because I'm going in on her if she didn't say shit." "Wait", I say. "You just came in from outside right? Why you didn't just grab something while you were out? But, you don't have to worry about saying shit to her because she don't have shit in the bag. She was running her mouth when I went over there earlier so I figured she was good for today." "Running her mouth to who?" Jazz asks. "I'm pretty sure you could have still asked her. Don't be like that." "So just be a fool huh", I say. "The same friend that was over there when I saw you over there was back over there. Coincidence or whatever. I'm pretty sure it wasn't job related, or if it was, she should have asked him to get her something. I don't work like that. If you got time to be talking to somebody, then you got time to ask them to get you something." "I feel you on that", she says. "But it's not that serious, Mase. She just talks to dude because he talks to her. I guess she trying not to be rude or whatever. He might have her number though, or she might have his. I don't know, but somebody has somebody number." "You know damn well if she gave him her number Jazz. Come on now, that's your cousin, not just some random chick you met in here. You don't just pass your number around do you? Right, don't even answer that. I don't know *what* they on but I'm not getting caught up in no bullshit. If she wants to fuck with Tom or whatever his name is, then that's great. I guess he saw me over there and wanted to put his bid in. I guess she like the conversation too because no guy is just going to be hanging around if he feels like it's no chance whatsoever. I understand you can't stop somebody from stopping by, but the vibe you give off will determine if they keep coming. Shit, I can't blame him for hanging around. She friendly like that." Jazz is laughing. "You tripping. It's not even like that."

Speaking of Toya, I can see her coming towards me while I'm talking. I wonder did they offer her a full-time position too. Not that I really care, I'm just wondering. Jazz has walked off at this point. "You acting funny now?", she asks. "No", I answer quickly. "I'm just seeing what's really going on. I think you doing a little more than you say you doing. I had something for you earlier when I came over there but you were occupied so I kept it to myself. So my surprise for you turned out to be a surprise for me." She has this surprised, but confused look on her face and I already know the explaining is coming up. "Okay Mase, what's on your mind? I can see that you got something you want to say. You can't even hide it because it's written all over your face. Ok, yes, Tom is super friendly and he probably trying to like me, but I don't look at him like that. Yes, he has my number too. I didn't give it to him on no get with type of shit either. It was more of the show me the ropes type of thing on my end. I didn't have any intentions of doing anything extra with him. He might have another motive, but that's something he has to deal with on his own. And why you care anyway?" "I'm just wondering", I say. "It looks like you loving the conversation to me. Maybe you just extra friendly, I don't know. I can't get caught up in no bullshit though. If you on some extra shit just let me know." Toya starts laughing. "Do I seem like the drama loving type of person?" "You want me to answer that?" I ask. "Serious", she says. You think I'm on some bullshit when I'm not. Don't worry about what somebody else do with my number. Worry about what *you* do with it. I gave it to you for reasons way different than what I gave it to Tom for. So stop bullshitting with it. "After hearing Toya's little essay, I tell her "okay, I don't want no bullshit." Not that it's a big deal if she *did* give him the number for her personal reasons, but I'm not participating in the bullshit when I see it from the jump.

I see Mack across the floor talking to a young lady so I tell him to come holler at me when he's done. Don P is in the area and sees me and congratulates me on becoming full-time. I just hope he put the word in so I can try and stay on day shift. Whatever weight his name holds, I don't care, as long as he put the word in. That's all that really matters to me. I can see Paul walking up the line too. I wonder if he has any say so about the full-time procedure. "You good?", Paul says as he walks by. "So far", I say. "I'll be even better f I can stay on day shift though." "Well", he says laughing. "That's a long shot, you know. Most people go straight to nights when they get switched over. That's just how the seniority thing works. The people with the most seniority get shift preference, which usually is days, and the people with less seniority usually be on nights. You have a few who have been on certain shifts for so long that they don't want to switch, but it's a lot of people that jump on a opening as soon as it becomes available. Like I said before, it's some rare cases where it just works out and the person stays on days. It's not going to be that much different on nights. Same procedures when it comes to the jobs. The people might be different than on days because it's younger people on nights. Be glad though, you get all the benefits now. Paid absences, vacation, and a piece of the profits with the profit sharing check. So you official now. Get off work and have a drink today. Them words Paul spoke to me sunk in for the rest of the day, and soon as I was off, I went straight to the store and got a double shot. Might as well celebrate. I'm back in the workforce officially now, with an increase. Life is good.

Chapter "It's On"

I text Sarah to tell her the good news and she instantly calls to stop from texting everything she wants to say. She's more excited than I am. I can tell by the tone in her voice. I can understand why she would though. She's seen me down and she's seen me up. She knows I deserve it. She also tells me we have to have a celebration drink when she gets off. I tell her I already started but I'll get something else so we can sip later. I guess I'm not that excited but I guess that I should be. It's a lot of people trying to get these jobs and I just happen to get one of them.

You get a different feeling when you are officially a full-time employee at my job. it's like you have a sense of relief because you know that now you have a little bit of leeway. You can't just be let go for any and every reason. As a TPT worker, you really don't have any room for error. You can be fired for whatever reason they feel the need to fire you for. The line of defense is very slim for TPT's. You have the union representation but they can't fight for you like they can for a full-time employee. That is the reason so many TPT's feel like they have to go above and beyond to prove their worth to the company. I have heard stories of TPT's coming to work sick, scared to go to medical, and so many other things that it's crazy. It's like they are intimidated by the company. I guess I *am* glad to have that burden off my shoulder.

I stop at the store to grab some tequila for the celebration later. I go to put my safety glasses in my bag and see the piece of paper with Toya number on it. I should throw the shit out the window, but instead I punch the number in my phone and send her a text. After a few minutes, she replies back "who is this?" After I tell her it's me she responds back "about time". I know she wasn't expecting me to hit her up today, or she probably was, after the shit that I was saying earlier. I ask her did they offer her full-time and she says not yet. I then tell her that they offered me full-time and I accepted it. She gives me all types of congratulations and then says we have to celebrate somehow. I let her know I'll keep her posted on a day. Like I been saying, I really don't want the headache right now.

When Sarah comes in, she is more excited than earlier. If nothing else, I know she got my back with whatever I do. I can't deny that. You need somebody like that to help fill in the blanks and keep the balance in your life. In the end, she'll probably end up as my forever.

I get out a little bit earlier the next day to make a breakfast run on my way to work. Being the nice person I am, I grab something for Toya too. I make sure it's something that I eat just in case she already got something. Hey, I'm not just going to throw my money away. I see Mack when I'm walking in and tell him I'm full-time now. His exact words are "aww shit, you gotta blow a blunt now. You officially in the house. You certified now". He also gives me his number to hit him up. I got some extra time so I figured I'll go give Toya her stuff before the shift start. Jazz is over at Toya's work area when I get over there. I speak and hand Toya her stuff. Jazz says a sarcastic "okay, I see you". Toya leans forward with her arms out for a hug and when I hug her she whispers in my ear, "today is the day." I pull back and look at her confused and she whispers, "no clothes". I can't even keep my reaction to myself and blurt out "oh shit, I have to pay attention then". I remembered that she told me when she told me one day she only going to wear her underwear under her jumpsuit, and today she finally did it. While I'm walking away I get a text from her asking me to watch and see if I can see her ass jiggle through her uniform. That's crazy. I'm definitely going to pay attention though.

When I get back to my work area, I just take some time to notice what everyone is wearing. Most people are wearing newer shoes, with most of them being Jordans or Air Max's. Even the ladies rocking them too. I guess they make a small deal about the shoe game in here. At least it seems that way. Even when I see people who don't work on this side, I notice that some be rocking the J's. I'm used to wearing my older shoes as my work shoes, but I can bang with the youngsters if I wanted to though. I have a nice shoe setup as well myself. I don't know if I'll ever rock my decent shit in here. Too much bullshit that can get on my kicks that might not come out. I might bring out a pair every now and then for show and tell. I like to keep my kicks crispy though so I don't know.

The bell rings for break and before I can even get away from my work area, her comes Toya. "You better not leave me at lunch time. And don't come with no bullshit either." She sounds a little bossy so I have to get this cleared up. "Is that your way of asking me? Because it sounds like you pretty much telling me what I'm gone do. Don't do that. You gone start asking me and not telling me. I'm still trying to make sure you not on no bullshit." Toya not really taking me serious, and I can tell when she says "ok, I got you" really quick, like she trying to shut me up. "I'm serious", I tell her.

"Make sure I don't have to look for you either. You know the time be moving." I make my way towards the bathroom and she goes on her way.

Since lunch will be coming soon, I do my usual stock up so I can have some downtime after lunch. I put together two bins of parts and take one over to Toya. When I get over there, I'm expecting her to be getting ready to leave out but she talking to Tom. I just laugh to myself. I don't say anything, I just set the parts down and made my way back to get the other container. I ain't even got time to worry about what she on. If she be outside, cool, if not, then the day will still go on as planned. As I'm putting on my jacket, I get a text saying don't leave me from Toya. I damn near want to rush up out of here to prove to her she will get left everyday messing around with me.

When I get to the door ready to walk out, I see Toya by the door talking with Tom. She sees me and instantly shuts down whatever conversation she was having. Jokingly, but seriously, I tell her she can stay in the building if she needs to. She doesn't say anything but her sighs and gesture say enough. "I told you it ain't like that", she says. "And I told you I'm not like that either", I tell her. "I'm not going to be a part of your fan club. You don't think that look crazy when you all up in his face then hanging with me? That shit feel crazy and we not even on that type of level. It looks messy, actually. But I guess you trying to decide what you gone do so you are weighing your options." I already know she fumed after that. "Options? What options you talking about? Tom ain't even a choice, let alone an option, but you keep putting him in that category." I interrupt her immediately. "You making it look like he more than an option. You already said he on your head but I guess you don't know how to spin people or maybe you don't want to spin him. Maybe I'll just talk to you outside of work so I don't feel like a fan. I don't want you to stop talking to your boy because of me. I ain't nobody." "See, now you on that bullshit", Toya says. "I already told you I'm not feeling him like that and you keep saying that shit. I'm not saying he not trying, but I'm keeping that shit simple and to the point with him. Oh, and he did ask were me and you talking. I told him a little bit."

We get to the store by this time and her answer is still in my head. "You told him yea, a little bit? What the fuck is that? I ain't ever heard an answer like that, and what guy is asking about another guy? That's different, but I'm starting to see that guys up in here are different. At least some of them. I'll never be used to the way they act, I guess." Toya is shaking her head laughing. "Oh my God, you crazy. You going overboard now. But you got a got a girlfriend anyway so you can't say nothing." "Wait right there", I say. "You still never asked me outright. You keep making these statements but never actually heard me say it out of my mouth." "I didn't have to ask", she say. "Your whole demeanor says you have a girlfriend. Then it took you so long to even hit me up that I knew you had one. I'm not saying I'm the coldest thing walking, but who just holds on to somebody number and not use it? So I put all that together and boom, you got a girlfriend. But since you keep playing around with it, do you?" "Yes, I do", I say. "For a couple years now. I just had to make you ask so you can officially hear it from me." "but I already knew that", she says. "But since you had to confirm it, whatever. I had my mind made up without you saying anything. And why you only get one shot for yourself? I need one now." We both laugh as I pull into the parking lot.

It's a larger than usual crowd outside today when we get back and I instantly feel like I'm on the watch by the paparazzi. I already know all eyes will be on us when we walk in together. I see Jazz outside talking to some chick and I already know Toya going over there before she go in so it really won't look like we were together. Perfect timing. But, soon as I think I'm in the clear, here go Jazz big ass mouth, "where ya'll coming from?" To make it worse, she didn't even wait for us to get in regular speaking range, so the few people standing outside just had to be nosy. Of course, Jazz had to introduce me to the girl she was talking to. This is the bullshit, but whatever. I really hate being introduced and all the bullshit but it is what it is. Toya tells Jazz we just rode out to get some fresh air and Jazz says "ummhmm", like yeah, whatever. This is the bullshit I tried to avoid.

The day is going pretty smooth and Larry comes up and asks had Don P told me anything new. I'm thinking he must've heard something, but he just says he was asking and just to keep coming until they tell me otherwise. Okay, that's what I was planning to do anyway, I was thinking. I definitely don't plan on asking if I'm getting sent to another shift. Don P already told me to ride it out, so that's what I'm gone do. I wonder did they say anything to Toya about her being full-time yet.

I'm in my own little zone when I hear what sound like arguing, but I'm thinking, it can't be that, not at work. After a couple of seconds though, I hear "bitch, if you was up on yo shit, you wouldn't have to worry about nothing." Ok, now I know it's not no playful shit going on so I look around to see where the commotion coming from. When I zoom in, I see two females standing, looking at each other like they about to square off. One is in the aisle and the other is still pretty much at her work station.

They exchange a few more words then the one in the aisle says she ain't got time for this at work. I'm thinking like, she already made a scene so keeping it low went out the window a few minutes ago. That was some talk show shit for real. Now everybody talking to the other girl, getting the story I guess.

Larry is walking up with a grim on his face. "I forgot to tell you that you every now and then you might witness or hear about some type of argument or something. You have all types of people from all over the place working together. Some of the same people that went to the same high schools and came from the same neighborhoods are all in the same place. With attitudes and feelings and all type of shit. So what you just witnessed was the side effects of that." "Damn", I said. "But to do that shit in front of everybody is some bullshit. They could have waited." "Well, they lucky if nobody spread the word", Larry says. "If it gets to the right people, one or both of them could be suspended. That's one thing that's not tolerated, and that's workplace violence. So it's a no tolerance policy. It's too much going on and people too crazy to be taking chance nowadays." I feel exactly where he's coming from because it's not like they search us before we come in here. Anybody can have anything on them and no one will know until something jumps off. This shit crazy.

After all the little talk show episode, I figured I'll take a load over to Toya and make maybe chill over there for a little bit. She better not be pre-occupied because if she is, she cut off the rest of the week. I can see that she's just sitting down when I turn the corner by her area. Shit, she not working either! "Must be nice", I say as I tap her shoulder. "Oh, hey boo", she says in her usual tone. "What's up, you were missing me and had to come see me? I already know, you don't have to answer." "Uh, we *are* at work Ms. Lady", I say. "So, I'm bringing you your work. And I was missing seeing you work, so yeah, I was missing you. Now get your ass to work. I came to chill though for a little bit, I can't lie." "I already know", Toya says with a grin.

From her actions, I already know Toya didn't hear all the commotion because she would've been asking all kinds of questions and shit. I'll get around to that in a minute. I asked her did she ask about becoming full-time and she told me that they said they'll get back y=to her. "Well just stay on top of it", I tell her. "In this business persistence and preparedness is key. If you stay on their heads they will know your serious, so that might have something to do with their decision. Not saying it will for sure, but it definitely can't hurt." "Trust me, I been on their heads about it", she said. "Don P probably tired of me asking and so is Paul. And since you told me that you got full-time, I really been on their heads. I'm not gone let them overlook me." As I'm replying, Jazz is rolling up on her cart and damn near jumps off before it even stops. Before she even opens her mouth, I already know what's coming. "Girl, it was two bitches about to fight over on the other side. The one bitch was all up on the other bitch like she was trying to do something but the other bitch just kept on working. Mase you should've saw it. It was right by where you work. I know if I saw it from my cart across the line you had to be right there!" I really don't want to get all involved so I calmly say "yeah, I saw pretty much all of it. The one chick was kind of oud but she walked off in the end. I guess she realized how dumb that shit was." By this point, Toya is amped up like she know the girl." Damn, you ain't tell me it was about to be a fight by you!"

"I was gone get around to it", I say. "I had to take care of the important stuff first and then deal with the recreational stuff. Your work and me asking about you being full-time was the first topic. The fight shit was second. But I was going to tell you, It's just that Ms. Info saw it and you already know she like CNN, ready to break the news. She just had good timing. Go on and flap off. I'll holler at you later. I know Jazz got all the info on who is who and what happened, so I'll talk to you later." They both start laughing as I walk off.

I make it back to my area and in my own little zone with my earbuds in, yes, I'm watching very closely for any supervisors. This young lady comes up saying something, so I take one of the earbuds out my ear. "You know they about to stop us from wearing those, right?" I'm looking at her semi-crazy because I know it has to be another reason other than that that made her come over here. She definitely came for something else. "You came over here just to tell me that" I ask. "Well that and that my girl said your kind of cute." "Oh yeah, kind of?", I say. "Where she at so I can know who stalking me?" "Damn", she says. "What if she didn't want you to know who she was?", she says, laughing. "Well, anyway, she over there with the light green jacket on. She was talking to me earlier and kept saying how cute you were so I told her I was coming down here to break the ice." This shit is crazy, I'm thinking. "First", I say, "I need your name then I need hers. I can't just be giving out info to strangers." She is laughing at this point. "I'm sorry, I'm Vickie and that's Karen over there, my sister. We not twins, but we got the same father, just different mothers. We lucked up and got in here at the same time. Our dad had a little hand in that though. He retired from here and still had his connects, so he got us in." "Must be nice", I say. "That shit pretty much over with now. They put you through the ringer and then back through the ringer to get in now. But I guess they have to do it like that to weed out some of the bullshitters." "Right", she says. "Well, I don't want to stop you from getting your work done, I just had to let you know somebody got their eyes on you." All I can do is laugh. "I got you", I say. "tell Karen I said what's up. I'm Mase, by the way. "Mase like the rapper?" she asks. I guess I'm gone hear this shit every time I say my name. "Yes, like the rapper. Mason, really." "Okay", Vickie says. "I got you."

I'm trying not to look over to where Vickie is gong but I want to see who this Karen chick is. I see Vickie stopping further down the line and instantly the female in the light green jacket comes into view. From down here she looks alright. Not in a bad way, but in a damn good way. Maybe tomorrow I will go down there and formally introduce myself. Maybe I'll wait until next week. Gotta stay with my motto though, never look thirsty.

Toya and Jazz are walking up while I'm working. "Great", I say. "You came to get your own shit. Now I don't have to walk over there for a while." Now you know that ain't about to happen", Toya says. "We were going to the vending machine and I told Jazz to stop by here to see if you wanted something. So, I'm actually being nice right now. You should appreciate it." "Ok, I guess I should, huh" I say. "Well get me some barbecue chips and some gum." "I asked if you wanted something, not a bunch of shit", Toya says. "Damn, so I'm not good for some gum" I need that after I eat the chips. I might kiss you or something." "What?" Toya says laughing. "I asked you about some snacks and you talking about kissing." "Just get the gum" I say. They walk off mumbling something to each other. I watch Toya to see if her ass is jiggling since she claims she only wearing panties under her jumpsuit. Okay, now I see what she was talking about. I send her a text telling her how good her ass looks but I still have to see it in person to really judge. Her response," we'll see, but I'm going to make sure I get that gum for later." I guess she thinking like I am at this point. I already knew she was going to get the gum anyway.

Mack comes up a little after they walk off and asks if I want to hit the bar after work. It's a few other people going, he says, and they hit the bar sometimes after work to just kick back and unwind. He says it's about ten minutes from the job so it won't really throw my trip home off that much. I tell him cool, just let me know where to pull up at. I send Toya a text telling her we going to have that celebration drink today after work. I guess she told Jazz too because she sends back "me and Jazz will be there". She asks if I'm going to the bar by the job a d I say probably so. I don't usually hang out a lot with co-workers, but since Mack put it on the floor I guess I can slide through. It'll give me a chance to see what Toya is about outside of work with that alcohol in her. Hopefully she still the same person and don't turn into something different. I know how that liquor can make a person clown.

Toya and Jazz finally come back with my stuff and Jazz lets it be known that Toya got me the gum. "You see that she got your gum so ya'll good for after work. And we will be at the bar so be ready. "Be ready for what?" I ask. "For your boo", she says. "This will be ya'll first little mini date." Toya is walking off at this moment, probably because Jazz put her on the spot. As soon as she is a few steps away, Jazz says, "you know she looking forward to seeing you after work. She be talking about you all the time, I swear. So you better not stand her up." "I'll be there", I say laughing. "If I asked her to go, why would I not be there? That's crazy." "Well, people do crazy shit", Jazz says. "I have to look out for my girl." "She grown", I say. "You don't have to watch over her like she a teenager. She good when she dealing with me." "Ummhmm", Jazz says, "I got you. We'll be over there though." When Jazz walks off I check the time to see how much time we got before we leave. Damn, I got to try and get my work done so I can have it set up for the next person that comes in.

    It seems like the day is going slower than usual. Maybe because the little drama that happened. I guess time stood still for those five minutes. It was only a short time but everybody talking about it probably just threw the day off. I take another bin over to Toya to make sure she is good for the day. She already has her stuff together and is just sitting, waiting on the bell to ring. I tell her I'll just meet her at the bar so no need to wait on me or anything. I see Mack on the way back to my work area and let him know I'll be at the bar about ten minutes after we get off. "What's the name of it" I ask. "Pauline's. You can't miss it. It's right on the corner", he says.

I take my time when the bell rings. Everyone is always rushing to get out the door and it just leads to a traffic jam in the parking lot. It's not like I'm going straight home anyway. I just remembered to text Sarah and let her know I'm going to the bar. That's just something I do.

When I pull up to the bar I can see that it's not too many cars, which is great. I really don't like the big crowds anyway. Plus, I really don't know who knows who yet so I don't just want my name out there. I see Mack getting out a car a few cars up from where I'm parked. Perfect, now I don't have to look for anyone I know in the bar. Toya is pulling up and hollers out the window to wait on her and Jazz.

The bar isn't the greatest looking place but it is real convenient and close to the job. I heard they have decent food so I might try something today. Maybe they can be my lunchtime spot sometime. I see Mack standing up by a table in the back. It's connected with a bench on one side so it's like a booth really. Once I get situated I realize this must be the spot that people hit for a quick after work drink. I see some familiar faces, but of course I don't know anyone's name really. I'm sitting with Toya and Jazz, so it's not like I'm actually with just someone in particular. The waitress comes over and takes our orders. I get a double shot of vodka and Jazz and Toya both get double shots of Hennessy. "Oh, so ya'll like that brown huh", I say. "That's my mood for today", Toya says." Jazz don't dink nothing *but* brown. I drink according to the mood I'm in." "Ok", I say. "I'll make sure I remember that for future references."

I can focus on my atmosphere a little better now that I'm settled in. I see Vickie and Karen sitting with another young lady at a table across the room. I tell Toya I'll be right back and to get my drink if it comes. Karen sees me walking towards their table and starts smiling and taps Vickie to get her attention. "You didn't say you were coming over here after work", Karen says. "Shit, I didn't know", I say. "This was decided a little before we got off. My boy asked me to come through so I was like fuck it. What's up Vickie? What you drinking?" I can tell Vickie is definitely caught off guard by my presence and for sure thrown off by me speaking directly to her. She says a shy "what's up", with a slight grin on her face. She says she'll take some wine. She probably usually drinks heavy but taking it easy today. I tell the waitress what she wants then tell Vickie I'll be back to check on her. Mack sees me walking back to my table so he motions for me to come over to where he's at. He is sitting at a table with three females and introduces me to all of them as his cousin. He also introduces me to a couple of guys seated at another table next to his. Of course, I won't remember anyone name. it takes time to lock people names in my head. Plus it's a lot going on in here and the drinks flowing and jukebox blasting.

    The drinks have already arrived by the time I get back to my table and Toya and Jazz have already started. Jazz says "I didn't know you knew Karen. She started around the same time as me. She was in assembly for a while but I guess she transferred. I see she still hang with that stuck up ass bitch Vickie." "Well, I just really met her today", I say laughing. "Don't nobody even like her, except a few guys, and that's about it. Prissy ass bitch. I remember her complaining when we were on the line about getting dirty. I was thinking like what the fuck, this whole place is dirty. That bitch need an office job." Me and Toya are cracking up at this point, and I ask Jazz is that the only reason people don't like Vickie and she says it's her whole demeanor. "She just has this attitude like she better than everybody else. At least that's how it seems to me." "So that's it", I say. "Just because she just stays to herself really and does her job and leaves, that make her stuck up? You on some bullshit Jazz and you know it. You really don't have a true reason to not like her." "Well, I don't need one" Jazz says. "And Toya, you better not fuck with her either. The one bitch Karen cool, but that other bitch Vickie? She gets no love from me." "Damn, you cold Jazz", I say. "She might be one of the coolest people around but you already got your perception made up about her. Stuck up might be a good way to be up in the job. it might be her way of keeping the guys up of her." "Don't nobody want her lame ass anyway", Jazz says. "The bitch ain't even from around here, she from the burbs." I tell Jazz she tripping and drink damn near my whole glass. It's only a double shot so it's not like a whole drink. I get the waitress attention and tell her to bring us another round. When she comes to the table with the drinks, she has an extra drink for me. "This is from the young lady over there", she says. I look over and Vickie is holding up her drink letting me know it came from her. I give her a thank you nod with a smile on my face. "Oh, the bitch buying you drinks too", Toya says. "What you go tell her when you went over there? it must've been something good because she all smiling and sending you drinks and shit." "You been hanging around Jazz too long", I tell Toya. "I didn't really say shit when I went over there, just spoke really. I don't know *why* she decided to send me a drink." "The bitch must like you", Jazz says. "Ain't no bitch gone just send somebody a drink if she not feeling him In a certain way. Hell naw, that bitch hate everybody and she like your ass", Jazz says laughing. I ain't ever heard about her fucking around with anyone at the job though, I can say that. Everybody I know that tried to holler at her said she was on some bullshit. And she like *yo* ass! Ain't that a bitch." I'm tripping off Jazz. "You crazy. You act like she can't like me or something. I know I'm not Denzel but I get a couple looks here and there." "Whatever", Jazz says. "I'm just shocked because I never even seen or heard about her liking nobody. She tells everybody that she has a boyfriend so they usually leave her alone after that. Then we get over here and the bitch send you a drink. That bitch ain't got no boyfriend, she just saying that to keep people off of her." "Well, apparently that shit working", I say. "You said you don't hear about her name ringing bells at work so it must be working. And drink ya'll damn drinks anyway. Stop worrying about her, since you say she ain't nothing." I decided to switch it up and stop fueling Jazz fire on Vickie, even though I know she likes me. i just switched the conversation and shot down all their talk.

After everyone finished their drinks, I told Toya and Jazz that we might as well head on out. I hollered at Mack for a quick second on my way out the door and let him know it was a straight little bar and I would definitely be back. I walk Toya and Jazz to their cars to make sure they get off safely. When I get to Toya's car she reaches her arms out for a hug, but when I go to hug her she gives me a kiss on the lips. The shit kind of through me off guard because my eyes were closed. Why they were closed? Hell, I don't know. I guess I close my eyes when I hug. Some crazy shit but whatever. I just wasn't expecting no kiss. After she does it she says, "see, the gum came in handy, didn't it?" I say "yeah, so did you not wearing no clothes under your uniform. I can definitely see the thickness."

As I'm driving home all I can think about is Toya. Pretty sure she probably driving, thinking about me too. She all right. If my situation was different then she might be perfect. But the world ain't perfect so it is what it is. I wonder how she gone act now after she gave me the little peck. She shouldn't be that different really. Not like we did anything extra, so she should be the same person and act exactly how she been acting.

My phone goes off as I'm driving and its Toya. The message doesn't say anything, it just says "tomorrow"? I don't know what the hell that means so I respond back "tomorrow what"? After a few minutes I get a message saying, "me and you, tomorrow"? Without even thinking, I send back "yeah, I guess". I don't even know what she talking about but, whatever. She probably just want to go have a drink or something, so whatever. She then replies "see you tomorrow." Now I have to think about that shit all night. Wondering what *she* talking about doing. Oh well, I guess I'll find out tomorrow.

When I get home, Sarah is already there with the dinner cooking. See, *this* is why her spot is solidified. It's so much that she knows and it's so much that she does on a woman's level that it's crazy. Perfect, really. I just look at her and smile and shake my head.

Chapter. Living Life

The drive to work the next day starts off hectic. I get out earlier than usual to stop for breakfast, but when I get to the freeway, the traffic is backed up. It's five in the morning, what the fuck! I'm not worried about being late, I just hope it clears up so I don't have to be rushing. I hate that shit. As long as I'm not late, that's all that matters. I get a text message from Toya saying "good morning" while I'm sitting in traffic. I reply back "oh, I'm on your mind huh? Good morning." This is the only benefit of being in a traffic jam. Being able to send messages with ease. Toya sends back "you been on my mind since yesterday. And when I woke up, you were still on my mind." I will admit, that brought a smile on my face. I was wondering would she just forget about yesterday, but she was well aware of what she did.

After a few minutes traffic starts to open up and flow smoothly. I can see police lights as I get closer to what looks like an accident, and once I pass the scene it is confirmed. I was looking for the other car that was involved but I guess it was just a one-car accident. Somebody tore their shit up on their own. I never understand one-car accidents. Oh well, long as the traffic back moving I'm good. I'll still make it around my usual time.

For some reason it feels different going into work today. I don't know if it's because of yesterday or not, but something just feels different. Maybe I'm just anxious about whatever Toya has in store for today. The whole just me and her thing is on my mind. I'm trying to figure out what exactly she has in store. It could be a list of shit or just one thing in particular. I hope she doesn't wait until the end of the day to tell me, whatever it is. I see Toya and Jazz standing together by Jazz cart so I go over and say what's up and give Toya her breakfast sandwich. She gives me a hug and whispers in my ear, "I can't wait until later". I want to ask her what she has planned but I just go along with it. I just hate surprises, especially when I already know I'm going to be surprised.

I get over to my work station and start getting ready for my day. Vickie comes up and says "good morning Mase". I tell her good morning and watch her walk back to her work station. Larry is watching the whole little exchange and comes up when Vickie walks off. "Well, she really don't even talk to people, including me, so I guess she feel a certain way towards you." "I don't know", I say. "I saw her at the bar yesterday and brought her a drink, that's all I did. Oh yeah, and she brought me a drink. Didn't really have a conversation or nothing. I heard she not friendly at all though. Or she just quiet and just deal with a couple people. Shit, I don't care if nobody like her, really. As long as she ain't no loudmouth or no shit like that, she good with me." "Okay now", he says. "I'm just letting you know in advance. But I feel you on that when you said you don't care if anybody likes her. That might be the best thing. Nobody can talk shit about her because it's no dirt on her name."

"Man", I say, "If it ain't nothing bad, it's all good with me."

The day is going pretty smooth so far, at a steady pace. I see Mack at break time and he asks me what did I think about the bar and I tell him I thought it was pretty cool. Lowkey and not too big of a crowd. Perfect after work location. I just have to try the food out. He tells me he usually hits the bar once a week, to just unwind and listen to some music, kick it with some people, and just vibe. I tell him to let me know when they hit it up because I might fall through.

I haven't really had time to talk to Toya about later, so maybe I'll chat with her after I take this load over there. As I'm getting my stuff together, I get a sense that someone is watching me. Not saying I'm psychic, but you can tell when someone is looking at you. I look around and catch eyes with Vickie. She just staring, and when she realizes I'm looking at her, she just smiles. I hope she not a crazy bitch. That's some crazy shit, though. Just to stare at someone? And watch them while they work? I don't know. I didn't even realize she worked this close to me until now. Her eyes are cold though. I can't tell the color exactly, but whatever they are, they'll definitely have you zoned in.

When I get over to Toya, she has company from her second favorite co-worker, Tom. Jazz is her first. Of course I'm just talking shit, but I already told her I'm not gone be a part of no bullshit. I speak to Tom and drop the parts off while giving Toya a nod. Before she can even really say anything, I'm already out of normal voice distance. I'm not about to wait around and see if he leaves or no shit like that. If he doesn't leave when I get over there, then apparently, she hasn't informed him to do so. That's the shit I be telling her but I guess she not seeing what I'm seeing. I can feel my phone vibrating on my way back to my work area, and before I even check it, I already know it's Toya explaining some shit. Soon as I press the button, I can see her paragraph message. It's basically saying why didn't I stay and he would've left, and all this other bullshit. I send her a message saying from now on I'll just talk to her outside of work. I also tell her that if she knows Tom got another motive and she not on the same page to let him at least know. Otherwise, it's gone be short talk at the job with me and her. I had planned on asking her was she riding out at lunch, but never mind that. That chance just left. I guess I'll do the solo thing today.

    Lunchtime is approaching so I'm trying to get myself situated to leave, and I see Vickie walking towards me. I continue to do what I'm doing because I need all my minutes before lunch, but I hold a quick conversation with her. "What you doing for lunch? She asks. "Probably going to the store", I tell her. "Why what's up?" "I don't know", she says. " I was wondering if you wanted a lunch partner. I mean, I can't ride out with you because I don't know you like that, but if you want to get something off the truck we can." "Well, I ain't no serial killer or nothing like that", I say laughing. "But since you don't know me like that I guess I can stay in and get something off the truck. For all I know *you* could be a serial killer. You always got that mean look on your face, looking like you ready to do something. I be like let me stay on her good side."

"Whatever", she says laughing. "I'm not really a mean person, I just stay to myself and let people think whatever they want. So you gone meet me at the truck?" "Yeah, I'll be over there", I tell her.

I didn't get another message from Toya saying anything else so I'm just gone assume she is doing her own thing for lunch, whether that's staying in or leaving out. I can't worry about that shit. She ain't said shit about it, and if I *was* leaving out it's not like I would be waiting on her anyway so, it is what it is.

The bell rings so I make my way over to the lunch truck to see what Vickie is talking about. On my way over there I get a message from Toya saying "wya", which means where you at. First off, I can't even believe she even texting me after not even really confirming anything or even really *talking* to me so far today. It's not like I even had the chance to see what she was doing, and when I did go to talk to her, she was busy. Nothing else was mentioned. She didn't think to ask when she saw me earlier so that's on her. I send back "still in the building, I'm not going out". She immediately calls. I figured she would probably do some shit like this anyway.

"Hello", I say nonchalantly. She immediately starts going. "Why the fuck you gone stay in today?" I can tell by her voice she pissed. "Hold on", I tell her. "First, calm the fuck down because you too hyped right now. And second, when you didn't say shit all day really, how am I supposed to know what the fuck you doing? I'm not a psychic. Why you didn't say anything about lunch when I came over there earlier?" Nothing but silence. At this point I can see Vickie over by the lunch truck so I end the conversation. "I guess you rushing out or whatever so I'll talk to you later." Toya responds back "bye man", and hangs up. I know she beyond pissed right now but she can't let that shit show in here so she gotta suck it up and hold it in. I bet she communicate with me a little better from now on.

I get to the truck and Vickie says "I was hoping you wouldn't stand me up and have me over here looking stupid. Thank you." "Come on now", I say. "I told you I was gone be here. So I'm here. Now what we gone eat?" "It's some deli sandwiches over there so I figured I would grab me one and a pop", she says. "I guess I'll grab me a slice of pizza", I say. "Hopefully it's not old. It's my first time eating pizza from off the truck." "You'll be all right", she says. "If you need to sue I'll be a witness and we both can get paid." "Oh, okay", I say. "That's good to know." When we get to the front of the line she says "I got it. I asked you to come over here so I got it. Don't worry, you'll get your chance to pay." I just laugh as we both go back towards our work area. I'm pretty sure it's some people noticing us walking but my face is newer than hers so it's noting that can be said. She starts telling me how people be looking at her and hating on her and all this other shit. Then she goes into how so many guys be trying to holler at her but she sees them in so many other females face, it's easy to turn them down. She said she doesn't even let them know why, so some guys take the shit personal and say she stuck up or think she better than everyone. "I see a lot of guys bouncing around from one chick face to the other too, but that shit doesn't affect me, so that's them", I say. "But why you choose to say something to me out of everybody else though? I mean, it sounds like you can have your pick in here. "She quickly interrupts. "I know, so I picked you. Me and Karen had been going back and forth about me not having a boyfriend for a while and we were joking that day when she came over there to talk to you about it. She said she gone find me a friend at work and somehow, we ended up talking about you and here you are. Yeah, I know we didn't know your name or nothing but all the initial shit was in place already." "So I was part of a game?" I ask. "No, not a game", she says laughing. "It just happened to play out in my favor." "How you figure that?" I ask. "You still don't know nothing about me except that I work here." "I know I don't see bitches in your face all day, so that's one thing", she says. "I know you haven't been working here that long but you'll be surprised how quick people move. You'll be thinking people knew each other before they started here how some people be. And I put all that together and took it as a sign that you have a girlfriend too, so you don't have to answer that. You act like you have a girlfriend without even saying it. It's a good thing though. Stay that way."

Wow is all I can think to myself after listening to Vickie. But at least I know where she is coming from. She checks the tie and says she guess she'll get back over to her area so she can be ready when the line starts. She tells me to put her number in my phone and maybe we can hang out sometime. I immediately send her a text letting her know to put my number in her phone also.

I am pretty much caught up on my work, so when the bell rings I take my time getting my next load ready. I have two bins full over here and whatever Toya is working with. I can take my two full bins now and that way I know she has more than enough parts. I catch Vickie watching me and give her a slight smile. Yeah, she might be a little crazy. The staring shit gone throw me off, I already know. I grab a bin and head over to Toya.

When I get over there I can sense that Toya is still mad at the lunch thing. She is silent when I get over there and didn't say shit until I ask about the parts. "It should be empty in about thirty minutes", she says. "So you not gone say nothing about earlier? You just gone come over here, grab the parts and leave, huh? You know you was on some bullshit, that's why you don't want to talk about it." Now I'm tripping because I can't even believe she is speaking on that now. "How was I on bullshit?" I ask. "When I came over here you were talking, so I politely went back to my area. You didn't even mention nothing about lunch at all. But it's my fault, I guess." "I thought we were riding out every day at lunch", she says. "I guess I was wrong." I can't believe she not acknowledging the fact that *she* was the reason for the miscommunication. "That was your fault though", I tell her. "I guess you wanted me to wait around or something. It don't work like that, baby. I'm not gone be blocking or stepping on anybody toes, I already told you that. So, I don't know what you gone do about your friend or whatever, but I'm not about to be looking crazy." "Whatever", she says. "You weren't looking crazy, and you probably had other plans for lunch anyway, that's why you didn't press the issue. Yeah, I heard about your little lunch date with the wicked bitch of the west. You spinned me for the bitch that everybody hate, out of all the bitches in here." I'm trying to figure out how she even know what the hell I was doing at lunchtime, but I'm tripping even harder because somebody actually told her. "So you got somebody watching me or something?" I ask. "Ain't no way you heard anything without somebody telling you. You didn't have a psychic feeling or nothing, somebody told you, like they were telling on me or something." Toya is laughing at this point. "You just got busted, that's all. You could've just told me you had other plans and I would've understood. You ain't have to lie about it. I'm a big girl, I can handle the truth." Now I'm getting a little on edge because first, somebody felt the need to tell her like it's a big deal, and second because she still hasn't told me who saw me. "If you not gone tell me who saw me then you might as well drop the subject. I hate it when people so eager to speak on somebody else word without telling the source. So if you feel you can't tell me for whatever reason, I understand. Just remember shit will never be the same between me and you. I'll feel like you rock with the enemy." "Don't go back saying I said nothing", she says. "I didn't have nobody watching you, that's not nothing I do. Tom said he was walking by and saw you and her sitting together. He said for a split second he thought it was me then realized it wasn't. I don't look shit like her, so I know that part was some bullshit. But that was pretty much all he said." "Tom?" I ask. "Why the fuck would Tom feel like he need to tell you about that shit? Oh yeah, I keep forgetting, he likes you, so that was right up his alley." Shocked that a dude will go that far to tell on another guy but that's what they do in here I guess. "Damn, you got people snitching on me", I say. I heard it's some suckas in here, but damn. Crazy part is if he knew the story he would've knew that she asked me at the last minute to go to the lunch truck. That shit was put together after I figured you were doing whatever else, so I told her yes. It wasn't nothing planned. But, that's your boy, I see, and apparently, he got you believing whatever. He got too much time on his hands."

This whole situation has me damn near about to explode. But I just know now to keep my distance from certain people. I guess he feel like he did something. Broad shit. Now Toya is trying to explain all the bullshit. "I didn't say it meant nothing , and I didn't say it changed the way I think about you either. Shit, I guess she trying to put her bid in. now I know why she brought you that drink. Me and Jazz said the bitch liked you, but you wanna act like you couldn't see it. Well, it's in the open now. So I guess ya'll exchanged numbers or some shit. Don't be bullshitting with me either." "You tripping", I say. "You the same person that got your special friends to show you the ropes around here or whatever bullshit reason he gave, but you wanna give me a lecture. What if she told me the same shit he told you? What if she said she gone look out for me? But that would be wrong huh? Don't be on no double standard, hypocrite shit." "That's not the same thing", she says. "I already told you that I'm not even feeling him like that, and no matter what his intentions are I already know where I'm drawing the line. So don't blow that up into something that it's nowhere near. And yeah, he probably told me because he likes me or whatever, but that's not gone change nothing on my end, trust that." "I hear you", I say. "I have to check on my work." "We still on for later too", she says. "And stay out that bitch face." "I'll see you later", I say as I walk off.

The Tom shit just won't go away out my mind. I don't know what he thought, that I was going to get cussed out or something? That's really some hating shit but I'm not gonna mention it. I'll just keep that in my back pocket as a memo. Now I know what type of person he is.

The line is down when I get back over to my work area. I see Vickie and Karen sitting so I ask them if they know how long we will be down and they said they heard it will be for a while. Something about a link broke on the chain or something. Perfect! Whatever the reason is, let it stay broke. I'll gladly take an easy day any day. Oh yeah, let me see if Toya still planning on whatever she had planned after work. I know how some people get when shit don't go their way, so I gotta see if she is canceling or not. I send her a text asking if we still on after work. After a couple minutes, she sends back "I guess so". I just laugh to myself after reading it. I guess she still salty because of earlier but she'll get over it. Larry comes and tells me that they haven't said anything about when the line will start so they want us to do some light housekeeping to pass the time. I definitely don't have a problem with sweeping on the clock. Easy money is always good.

Vickie comes down while I'm cleaning and asks what am I doing after work. I tell her that I got a couple errands that I have to run and I ask her what's going on. "I might've wanted to go have a drink", she said. "So I was seeing if you wanted to be my drinking partner but you busy today." "Yeah, today is a bad day but I'll take a rain check." "Well just let me know when you ready", she says. I watch her as she walks away. Vickie definitely has a nice shape on her. It's crazy that nobody really likes her and she has so much to say to me.

The line has been down for over an hour and everything is as clean as it can get. People are sitting and talking and just relaxing. What else can you do? It's only so much cleaning that can be done. Larry is talking to Don P and a couple other TL's off to the side. I guess they are discussing what's about to happen or whatever. Shit, I remember Mack telling me that they have been sent home before when the line went down. I hope today is one of those days too. When the huddle or meeting is over, Larry comes over and tells everyone to check their area and if it's clean, they can leave. Damn, it's still over a hour before we would've got off. I guess that works out great for whatever Toya got planned. I send her a text asking if they leaving early. She says they telling them now so she'll text me when she gets outside.

My parking space I got this morning was the best I've had since I been working here. I guess me staying in for lunch was a good thing after all, because when I walk outside, I'm right by the door. I go hop in my ride and wait on Toya to text me the plan. I see her and Jazz walking out so I'm assuming she will be contacting me once she gets to her car. She calls me when she gets to her car and asks if I know the area. After asking why she tells me she wants to go to a lowkey spot to eat and have a drink. Not the spot that the people from the job go to though. I tell her I know the area pretty well and we can just ride until we decide on something. We *did* get off early so most places should be empty. After riding for about ten minutes, I pull up at a little bar that barely looks open. They have food specials on the sign out front so this is it. I tell Toya to park and we both go in.

You can tell by the atmosphere that they really don't get too much business during early hours. We are literally the only people in the place besides the bartender and I guess the person doing the cooking. They tell us the rush usually comes after people get off, especially for happy hour. We take a table in the back still. They have a jukebox but the selections are very limited. Mostly mainstream and songs out of movies. We order some wings and a couple of vodka shots. I see Toya getting a little quiet so I break the ice. "So what's up T? You got me all by myself now." "Yes, and that's how I wanted it", she says. I could tell Toya had a nice figure even with her uniform on but she got these tights on now and I can really tell. I reach over and rub her thigh while saying "this thickness is my weakness". She smiles and says "well, I know CPR, so if you pass out you good". The perfect girl but the timing is a few years off. That's how it usually is though.

We have a few more shots and I can tell that Toya is feeling a little buzzed because she scoots her chair closer to mines and sort of leans over towards me. "I already know you can't be mines", she says. "It's messed up because I really like you and I know you like me. I don't want to just work with you, though. I don't want to just see you at work and not see you any other time. But I know I can't see you how I want to either, because your time is limited. Just be honest with me and we'll be all right. You don't have to worry about me dealing with nobody else at work, either. Nobody. I might chit chat with some people but that shit stops right there. No further. Hell, people already saying shit anyway about us so it's not like it's a secret." "You talking about Tom?" I ask. "No, not him", she says. "This girl I know said she saw me talking to my boy the other day so she didn't stop and talk and when I asked what he looked like she described you. So people pay attention even when you don't think they are. I think we look good together actually. You don't think so?" "I mean, I ain't never saw us together so I can't answer that", I say. Toya grabs her phone and says "take a picture so we can see".

"We don't need no pictures", I say laughing. "We can visualize it." "Boy, whatever", she says. "I ain't about to do nothing with your picture. You ain't gotta worry about being all on the internet. I ain't gone blast you." "I ain't worried about that", I say laughing. "I'm just talking shit. I know that's not your style." We take the picture and I ask to look at it and say "yeah, we look pretty good, I guess." Toya asks me what time is my curfew and I give her a look like what is that. "Don't play", she says. "You might not have a curfew but what time you have to be home?" "Not too late", I tell her. "What else you trying to do though", I ask. Toya gives me this look like she wanna say something then says "naw, I better let you go before I have you out too late. I might mess around and really get you in trouble today the way I'm feeling." "And how you feeling?" I ask. "Or should I already know that", I say as I rub her thigh, but this time I go a little higher and closer to the inner part of her thighs. "Now you know you tripping", she says. "You been to Paradise before? Cause' if you keep that up you gone end up in Paradise. After that your life will never be the same." "Really?" I ask. "I don't think I ever been to Paradise. That sound like some movie shit." "Yeah, it's some movie shit", she says laughing. "But it's not your regular kind of movie. This shit off the charts. I'm telling you, it will mess your life up." "Whatever", I say. "I hear you talking." I rub her thigh again but this time I touch the innermost part of her thighs. She adjusts herself in her seat so I can really get a good feel. I can feel the heat through her leggings as she whispers, "see what I'm talking bout'. Paradise." I'm beyond geeked at this point and a part of me is saying take her somewhere and knock her brains out, but the other part of me is saying take it easy. Whatever is meant to happen will happen. Toya reaches over and grabs me while saying "I think you feeling what I'm feeling." I have to switch the shit up because I don't even have time for the extra shit. "I'm definitely feeling exactly what you feeling", I say. "But I don't have time for that right now. You already knew that anyway, that's why you talking shit. We'll eliminate this stop next time. We can eat and drink anywhere." "Okay", she says. "Come walk me to my car." When we get to her car I give her a hug and a kiss on the lips. I also grab her ass at the same time. "You gone keep on", she says. "I'm telling you, one you go to Paradise your life will never be the same." "I hear you", I say. "You might just give me the key to Paradise and I can visit whenever I feel like it. Let me know when you make it in." She gets in her car and pulls off.

I already know all I had to do was say the word and Toya was ready for whatever. She probably thought I was gone jump at the chance too but that's why I told her we'll just wait. Make the anticipation even greater. She *is* something else, I must say. I'm pretty sure Paradise is too.

Just when I think I got the situation out of my mind, I look down and see Toya name as my phone is ringing. "Yes", I say as I answer. "Don't you wanna make sure I make it home safe?", she says. "You already know I'm buzzing and I don't want to get a ticket. It'll only take like fifteen minutes to get there, I think." "What you mean, you think", I say. "You know where you stay, don't you? You not that buzzed. But I guess I can make sure you get in, I guess." "Thanks", she says. "Call me if I drift through the lanes." I hang up and pull up on her a few blocks away and wait on her to pull out so I can follow her. If she sober enough to do all this then I'm pretty sure she could've made it home. I don't know how far she stay from here, but she said it's only fifteen minutes. Maybe she got another motive? For some reason, I think she *does* have another motive. I'll play her little game though, make sure she get in safe.

    I check the time to see what type of time I have t work with. Damn, I just remembered that we got off early so it's actually not even time for me to be off yet. I still text Sarah to see how her day is going and how she's doing. She still has about 2 hours before she is off.

    Toya pulls into this apartment complex that I've driven past before but never knew anyone who lived there. I follow her around a few corners and we end up in the back by a small lake or something. She parks and I pull up beside her. After a few minutes of waiting for her to get out, I get out and go over to her door. She is just sitting there, listening to her music. "I was waiting on you to come over here just in case I fell", she says laughing. "I don't know if I'm good enough for them steps. You should let me get on your back." Now I been drinking to so I'm just not sober, but I still tell her to "come on". Of course I take advantage of the situation and hold her by her thighs as she has her arms around my neck. "You love this don't you", she says as I walk up the stairs. "The one with the welcome mat is mines." She pulls her keys out her purse and hands them to me as I help her down. "The one with the yellow key ring."

I open the door and I'm not even surprised by the way her place is laid out. Pretty much the way I pictured it. I could tell Toya was a neat freak by the way she was at work and it definitely shows at home. Everything is a certain way and in order. It damn near looks like a model apartment. She puts her things down and says "thank you" with her arms outstretched like she waiting for a hug. Of course I give her one, but this time she holds me a little longer and just looks into my eyes before she gives me a peck on the lips. I let my hands do some body research and grab her ass. She pushes me away laughing and tells me to make us some shots with the liquor out the freezer while she gets in the shower. I really don't need another shot, neither does she, but I pour us two anyway. Not quite a full shot, just something to top off what we've already had. I guess she has something else on her mind right now.

When Toya comes out the bathroom she has on this sundress/gown that's showing all of her curves. She tells me there's a towel and washcloth in the bathroom for me to freshen up. I had an extra t-shirt that I keep in my bag just in case so that came in handy today. After I'm done, I come out with my shorts on that I wore under my jumpsuit and t-shirt. "Where your clothes at?", she asks, laughing. "Well, I don't just have extra clothes with me at all times so it is what it is. You want me to put my other clothes back on?" "Hell no", she says. "I guess I can behave myself. I just have this weakness for chocolate and you looking like a Nestle bar right now. I'm not gone keep you too long, but I wanted a massage." "Ok, so where you want that at, out here?" "No", she says. "We can go to the room for that so I can lie down." She heads towards the bedroom as I follow behind her admiring the view.

I bring a couple more shots with me as I head in the bedroom. I'm not a mind reader but I pretty much know what's on her mind. I have a little over a hour before I have to be leaving so whatever she on needs to be in motion.

When I get to the bedroom, Toya is laying on her stomach on the bed with her head resting on her arms. I take a quick look at her body and say "damn, you juicy". Toya is what you call extra thick. And the little dress or gown she wearing lets that be known. "You gone lay like that or can I move what I have to move to do what I need to do? I ask her before getting started. "I'll help you out", she says while lifting the dress over her head. She then turns back on her stomach and hands me this warming oil to use. "So you just got the oil on standby", I say laughing. "No, silly", "it's not even opened yet. You will be the first to use it on me."

I start from the bottom of her feet and slowly massage her feet and move up to her ankles and calf. She tells me how soft my hands are and I tell her to be quiet and relax. I massage both legs and move to her thighs. She has her eyes close at this point and I know she is in a zone. I work my hands from the outer to inner thigh a few times then I slowly but firmly massage both of her ass cheeks. I was hesitant at first, but when she didn't stop me, I didn't think it was a problem. I go from her butt cheek to her inner thigh a few more times then I go to her back and shoulder area. I can tell she thought I was going to touch Paradise by the way she moved her legs apart when I was rubbing her thigh. "Can you tell how tense I am?" she asks. "Yes, your whole body is tense", I say. "well, I haven't had one of these in a while", she says. "It was overdue. This shit feel so damn good." After doing the lower part of her back, I go back to her butt cheeks. This time I go from the outer thigh to the inner thigh, real slow. When I get to her inner thigh she moves her legs open a little bit more so I run my fingers slowly across Paradise. I can feel the heat as my fingers move slowly across her. After rubbing Paradise for a few seconds, I go back to her cheeks and then outer thigh. She is re-positioning herself as I move my hands back towards her inner thigh and touch Paradise again. "You something else", she says. "Naw, *this* something else" I say as I slightly push one finger in Paradise. I play around with her for a few more seconds then I turn her over and pull her on top of me. we kiss and feel on each other for a few more minutes and then I tell her I have to be going. She tells me she will buy breakfast in the morning and gives me a kiss before I leave. When I get to my car, it takes me a minute to process everything that just happened. I really don't know what to think right now. I know she was ready but the timing was off. No need to rush it though. I already know what she on. I just wonder how she gone act at work now.

    I try to remember the way I came in the complex as a reminder on how to leave back out. I'm pretty sure I'll be back out here so I make mental landmarks so I'll be able to find my way next time. When I get to the freeway, I fire up a cigarrello for the ride home. I call Mack to see what he got going on and to chop it up. I ask him how the women are at the job to get his opinion. "I don't really trust none of them", he says. "I might deal with them at work, but I don't really deal with them outside of work. I got my own thing at home going on so I really don't have time for the extra shit.

I might deal with one of them a little more than others, but I keep that shit at a certain level. You must've hollered at something." "Not really", I say. "I just wanted to see how they be acting. Ole' girl gave me her number though. The chick that started with me, and the other chick that work down from me." "Vickie? I had saw her down there so I figured something was going on but I ain't know that! She been dissing motherfuckers for years. As far as I know, she ain't never messed with nobody at the job. if she did, that shit was extra lowkey. If you got the number you a lucky dude. That bitch don't like *nobody*." "That's the same shit everybody else be saying", I say. "She might be one of them crazy ones. I might hold off on that number." "I don't know", Mack says. "It's different up in there with some women too. Some of them think you about to take care of them or some shit like that so they be on some other shit. You got a few that's on some real shit too, though. The old heads got a lot of the younger females heads fucked up too. They be the main ones on that pocket reaching and got a lot of chicks heads already on that shit. Then they try and run that same game on younger cats and the shit don't go the same. It's some young ones pocket reaching too, though. You gotta just watch what's going on and weed out the bullshit." I'm laughing after listening to Mack breakdown everything. I tell him I'll holler at him tomorrow.

Chapter: Playing It Smooth

I get home, hit the shower, and chill ot and wait for Sarah to get in after work. I've had an incredible day in more ways than one. I'm mentally drained but physically charged. Sounds backwards I know but that's how it is. I'm not physically tired but it's so much on my mind that I damn near got a headache. I can't wait until Sarah gets here so she can rub my temple. I'm still thinking about Toya though. I'm not gone hit her up though because she might be busy or something. She not expecting my call anyway. I already sent her a message saying I made it in safe, so that's the main thing. I'll talk to her about everything else tomorrow.

I wake up earlier than usual the next day. My alarm isn't even close to going off yet. Sarah asks if something is wrong because I'm up so early. "Naw, I'm just wired up, I guess", I tell her.

I guess I'm just anxious to see how the day plays out after my little episode with Toya yesterday. Since she's up, Sarah makes me a breakfast sandwich to eat on the way. I end up getting out a little earlier than usual.

As soon as I get into work I run into Vickie, who is on her way to her work station. When she sees me, she stops and gives me a hug and says "good morning sweetie". I grab her bag and tell her "I guess i can carry this for you since we going the same way." "Why, thank you", she says. "This the first time somebody even offered to carry my bag." "As many people that be on your head?" I say. "I'm sure you got plenty offers." "Nope", she says. "They don't realize it's the simple shit. They think everything is complicated or that you gotta involve money with shit. I'm not like that. I got my own shit so a guy is just a helper to me. Not knocking anybody that goes the easy route, but that's not me. a lot of these niggas be lame anyway. They don't even know how to approach a woman." After hearing all that all I can say is "I feel you". I could pretty much see how a lot of dudes be acting already. I had heard about the women too from people I know that worked in the plant. It's a different type of life.

I set Vickie's bag down by her work station and tells her I'll be hollering at her throughout the day. People have this crazy perception of her and she really only reacting to the way people come off on her. I'm not one to really speak on the next man either, so whatever people think is working for them, hey, more power to them.

My phone goes off as I'm getting situated and it's a message from Toya saying, "good morning boo". I send back "good morning" and continue what I was doing. After a few minutes, I get another message from Toya. She tells me how she had a nice time yesterday and how she wished I had stayed longer. She also says she wishes she could get a massage every week. "We'll figure that out", I text back. I'm looking around and notice that the last operator didn't leave a lot of stock for me to start my shift with. I guess they were rushing to leave. It's still some bullshit. The worst way to start your day is rushing. That sets the tone for the day. Larry comes up and says he thinks the last shift left early because a lot of people have to get their work stations in order. I really don't give a damn about anyone leaving early, that just means you had time to get the shit together before you left.

I already know Toya probably told Jazz about yesterday. I just feel it. Plus, that's her closest homegirl so I already know they had their little girl talk. That's expected. I catch Vickie looking down towards me and when we catch eyes, she just smiles. I can already tell that Vickie is ready for whatever. As I'm working, I see this older cat walking up the line speaking to people, mostly females. He stops a few stations down from me and I can hear him tell the lady, "whenever you ready, I got your money". "I ain't thinking about you H", the woman says. "You'll mess around and have a heart attack dealing with me. You need more than them pills." Well, whenever you stop being scared, let me know", he says. He gives me a nod while walking past and says "they want the money but they don't really want the money. How you gone act like you need something and act like you don't need it at the same time? These young girls crazy. I tell em' I'm gone get me a old one and forget about all of they young asses. They lazy in the bed anyway." I'm laughing at him as he continues. "I'm serious. I had this one twenty-two year old and she was talking so much shit I *had* to see what the fuck she was about. I got grandkids her age but she was so persistent. We get to the room and all she want to do is smoke and do doggystyle. She don't want to get on top or nothing. Lazy. Soon as I was done I got the fuck up outta there. Gave her some money for her tank and never fucked with her again. I know she was probably wondering why I gave her an extra fifty. That was for her to actually leave me the hell alone. Like a parting package. She usually hit me up during the week for gas money so that's a payment in advance. When she call next time, I won't answer. She too young to be that lazy in the bedroom. I can get an old woman if I want some lazy shit." "I feel you", I say. "The younger ones be all talk and then be scary when they get behind them closed doors. Some of them know what they doing though, I have to admit. You just have to find the right one." H, or whatever his name is, is checking out something inside of the vehicle. I guess he has something to do with the painting or something because he is taking pictures and feeling on the paint like he's seeing how smooth it is. After looking at the frame, because that's pretty much all it is, he walks off. I look down the line at the lady he was just talking to. At least he got flavor. She all right! Larry walks up laughing and says "I see you met H. his name is Hurley but everybody calls him H. he got probably like thirty years in here. He an inspector. He might do some work every once in a while, but mostly he working on the women." "I see", I say laughing. "He don't look like he working hard at all. That's probably why he haven't retired yet. Plus he probably getting top dollar and love coming in here looking at them young girls. He already said he paying them, so that's not an issue either." "Well, you got guys like H who been here forever so they don't have a problem spending fifty here and fifty there. That's all they know. A few of them told me they put money aside just so they can be ready when they gotta spend something. I can't be like that. If we involved with each other, that's one thing, but to just be throwing money away, I ain't doing that. Like I said, I'm sure some of them getting something in return, but I just can't go that route. You'll see how some of the old cats be, trust me."

To each its own is all I'm thinking when Larry walks off. I ain't never been a trick so why would I start up in here? That shit is not pimping, that's simping. Like an older ca once told me, either you pimping or you simping, you can't do both. I'm not mad at H though. If what he's doing is working for him, then I guess I'm happy for him. Somebody gotta do it.

The first break bell rings so I make my way to the truck to see if I can grab me something to drink. I see Toya and Jazz walking together on the opposite side of the aisle. Toya hollers across the line "so you getting my breakfast today"? first I feel kind of surprised that she even put me on blast like that, then I realize she probably not even thinking about who listening or none of that. I nod my head yes but I don't say anything. I'm not about to add to the attention. It's too much space in between us and I'm not about to holler back and forth. I hope she not in a rush either because I have to stop at the bathroom first. I see Tim by the bathroom talking to some young lady. He gives her something folded up before she goes into the bathroom. I'm not a genius or anything, but it definitely looked like he gave her some money. He gives me a "what's up" nod as he walks away. I laugh to myself thinking that's a young H in the making. I haven't been working here long, but I can tell Tom thinks he's some kind of player up in here. From the way Toya say he be talking, to the way he be acting, I can tell. Always up in a chick face. And he keep that damn brush with him, even when he trying to get his game on. That shit I don't understand but hey, I guess the chicks dig it.

    I get over to the truck and Vickie is walking away as I'm walking up. She whispers, "hey boo" as we're passing each other and I give her a wink. The look on my face must've let it be known that she said something to me because when I get to the truck Toya says "yo girl must've said something". "Why you say that?", I ask. "Cause I was watching you and I told Jazz I bet she say something to you and she did. If she didn't, why were you smiling when you passed her? So I know the bitch said something." "I wasn't even really smiling though", I said. "and why you watching me anyway? What did you think you were going to see?" Now she is on the defensive tip. "I was just seeing what you were going to do when ya'll saw each other. Long as you didn't give the bitch a hug. I would've really been pissed. I know I don't have the right to, but that shit would've pissed me off, especially to see it right in my face." Jazz is looking surprised at Toya. Maybe she hasn't told her about yesterday. Jokingly I say, "you wanna be my girlfriend T? Cause' that's what you acting like now." Toya instantly snaps back. "No, nigga, you already got a girl so I can't be that. And if I was your girl, you wouldn't be smiling at no other bitches." Jazz of course has to add her two cents. "I guess she told you." "Jazz, please don't gas her up", I say. "She already running on ninety-three octane right now. She don't need no more fuel." "You want a hug T", I say, pulling Toya towards me. "Nope, don't try and touch me now", she says. "You wasn't thinking about me when you were smiling in that bitch face, so don't touch me now." We at the front of the line at this point so I look at Toya, waiting on her to keep her word and buy my breakfast but she tells the lady she's paying for hers. I can't hold back any longer so I say, "you wasn't acting like that yesterday". Jazz was walking a little ahead of us but I know she heard me say that because she instantly turned around. "What ya'll do yesterday" "Nothing", I say. "We had a drink after work." I'm walking towards my work area at this point and Jazz says , "don't worry, I'm pretty sure I'll her about ya'll drink after work." I already know that because her girl will probably fill her in.

As I'm loading my parts, I think about how pissed Toya was when she saw me talking to Vickie. Them feelings came out today. If I would've hugged Vickie, Toya probably would've blurted out something, unconsciously. I'm glad I didn't go all the way with her yesterday. She would've clowned for real. I know Jazz gone be on her head about what happened too, but nothing really happened. I gave her a massage and we took some shots. She gone leave out the other part, I'm sure. Long as she keep the important business between us, we good. If some shit get back to me then I know where it came from.

I see Don P walking around, talking to a few people. I wonder if Toya been asking him about being full-time. Hopefully, she stay on his head, but that's something she has to take care of. If she really wants the spot, she'll stay on him. He comes down my way and I can hear him asking people how their doing, and just greeting people and doing the stuff you want your supervisor to do. He asks me how I like the job and that's pretty much it. I guess it's not too much to say. I mean, I already know my schedule, I'm full-time, and I'm on the shift I want. I really don't have nothing to ask him anyway.

I notice a young lady working across from me on a job that isn't hard, just tedious. A guy walks up and starts talking to her, and she starts falling behind on her work. I'm thinking that he's gonna help her at least do something on her job, but he just keeps talking and she keeps working like it's nothing. To top it off, instead of helping, he moves back so she can finish her job and keeps talking.

What the fuck is she thinking? I laugh to myself and keep doing my job. that shit crazy. If she don't know any better though, what can you do but shake your head.

I get a text from Toya asking what's up for lunch so I send back "I'm chilling". Every now and then you have to throw in the remix. She sends back "ok". I'm laughing as I look at it because I know she wanted to write a paragraph but probably didn't feel like writing it. She didn't expect my reply though, I bet that. She already probably thinking Vickie on my head so she feeling like she gotta be on her shit. Speaking of Vickie, I send her a text saying she look sexy working and she send back maybe she'll role play for me one day. Hell naw, I say to myself. I was actually just bullshitting when I sent that message. Something to pass the time, and she came back with that. Now I know.

Mack and another guy walk up and start talking to some older ladies who are working a few stations down from me. I haven't really noticed until now that I work around mostly females. Everywhere I turn, I see at least two or three females. It's like being at a black college or something. I'm pretty sure it's more men than women working in here, but in this area, the women definitely outnumber the men. Mack and the other guy stop to holler at me on their way headed to wherever they're going. Mack tells me about the lady he was just talking to. Said they used to call her three hundred because that's how much she was charging. "Damn, just like that?" I ask. "She just let it be known that's what she on?" "Not outright", Mack says. "She just used to be talking shit like she need three hundred before she get to the hotel. This was before I started working here though", Mack says. "My mans JP said he was here when she was on that tip." JP is the other guy's name that's hanging with Mack. I hit him with a "what's up" as Mack continues telling me about the lady. "So, you trying to get her to come out of retirement?", I joke with Mack. "Hell naw", Mack says. "She got this little business that write grants and I'm trying to start this non-profit organization for teenagers. You know, do something different." "Oh ok", I say. "Something positive." "Right", he says. "The youngins definitely need something positive, and I think this will be something that can help them in all areas, from school to life issues." "Well", JP says, "I was thinking about asking her if she still working, really. Shit, she still got that ass. That shit ain't went nowhere." I start laughing as they walk off. Three hundred? Man that shit better be for the whole week. Mack comes back and asks if I'm rolling out at lunch and I tell him I might as well. He then jokes and says, "unless you riding with ole' girl". I start laughing and ask, "who you talking about?" "Nigga, you don't think nobody see you when you and her go out? I know if I see you then a few other people *have* to see you." "Like some paparazzi shit", JP says. "People love to see some shit and love to tell some shit. This shit like a little city, I'm telling you. I already know Mack told you how it is." "Yea, he put me up on it", I say. "I'll holler at ya'll boys."

    JP seem all right. Don't really know him like that, but he seems like he all right. If he hanging with Mack, I'm pretty sure he on point up in here. Mack didn't fuck with too many people in high school so if he fuck with him then he must be all right. I'm still tripping about the three hundred lady. She probably was wilding back in the day. Now she all quiet kike she a new person. Well, I guess she is a new person. That shit was years back.

I still got time to take a load to Toya before lunchtime so I hurry up and get it together so I can drop it off. She is sitting down, as usual, when I get over there. "This what you do most of the day, huh", I say. "Boy, you know I do my work so don't even start", she says. "I keep up with my job and when I get ahead, I chill. You already know the process. Anyway, we getting a drink today? I need one. I was stressed out earlier. That's why you should've stayed longer yesterday. I'd be more calm and relaxed." I give her a sarcastic look that says "oh, really", and she understands it without me saying by responding "yeah, you should've stayed a little while longer. But, we got time for that. I been waiting seven months so I can deal with it." "Seven months?", I say. "I'm proud of you. that's control right there. Let me get back over here. I'll see you outside." I hurry off and get ready to leave out for lunch.

When the bell rings I am already damn near at the gate. Toya is calling as I'm getting to my car and I tell her where I'm parked at. She gets in and instantly kicks her shoes off. "You comfortable?" I ask. "Yep, and you should be glad I am", she says. "I already told you I don't like people like that, so you should feel special." I'm still thinking about what she said earlier so I bring it back up. "Were you telling the truth earlier when you said seven months, or just talking shit?" "I was telling the truth", she said. "Why would I lie about that? Well, I know why somebody would lie but I'm not lying. That was my last boyfriend and it was right after my birthday so I remember that shit like yesterday. I been just chilling since then. You came the closest though, I will admit." "Why me?" I ask. "I'm pretty sure you ran across a few guys over the past few months, so what happened?" By this time, we pulling up to the store. "Hold that thought", I say. "Don't forget my Reese's", Toya says. "I already know that", I say as I walk in the door. I grab a few snacks and a couple shots and head back to the car. "Okay, so what were you saying?" I instantly get back to the convo. "You just gotta know, don't you?" Toya says. "But naw, I met some guys of course, but they just didn't appeal to me, really. After going out a few times

I just said fuck it, I'm chilling. Ya'll be to stupid. Not at first but as time goes on. So I hope you don't be stupid. You gone send me back to hibernation." "Damn", I say laughing. "I get all the pressure and I'm gone get all the blame. That's messed up." "It be like that sometimes", she says as she drinks her shot. "Somebody gotta get the blame and I chose to open up to you, so if I shut it down it's your fault. And I already knew what I was getting into with you, so maybe this girlfriend thing makes it easier, I don't know. It lets me keep my feelings at a certain level. I wasn't planning on doing no shit like this either, but your whole vibe or whatever, that shit just got to me." "I wasn't even trying to get to anybody, really" I said. "I was planning on coming in here and doing my hours and leaving. That's why I keep to myself. This extracurricular shit just happened like a movie. "We pull into the lot as we both finish off the little shots and Toya says "well, I like this movie so far." She leans over and gives me a peck on the lips after I park. "You like the movie so far, huh" I say. "Yep", she says, as she gets out and walks towards the entrance. I see a couple of people going back in and laugh to myself thinking about the shit Mack and JP was saying about other people paying attention to what other people doing. So I'm pretty sure that somebody saw me and Toya. She says in a voice that only I can hear as we are going back in the door, "you still owe me for yesterday." "I got you", I say. I know she not gone let me forget about it.

Tom is standing in the hall as we walk in with a coupe of other guys. Me and Toya speak to the group as we walk by. I'm sure Tom will feel them in on whatever he thinks is going on between me and Toya. He like to tell shit like a female so I know he can't wait to run his mouth. Toya must be feeling the vibe because she tells me "I guess he gone tell his boys I'm the one he tried to talk to." "Maybe, maybe not", I say. "He wasn't successful so it really ain't nothing to tell. he might tell them you and me fucking around though. I'm expecting that. He seem like that type. He already showed you that!"

We go our separate ways to our work areas and I check the time and see we sill have a couple minutes left, so I stop down by

Vickie. "What you eat for lunch?" "I made grilled chicken salad last night so I brought that in." "You made it?" I ask. "Yes, that's some easy shit to make", she says. "I might bring you some in next time, or I might just make you some for yourself. It's better than the shit they be selling at these Coney Islands." "Well, I'll be waiting", I say, as I walk down to my work station.

H is talking to another young woman across the aisle from me as I start my job. I guess he trying to set something up for the future or just paying his dues. I see him hand her some money before whispering something in her ear. I guess she already on his payroll. They don't like them old men but they like that old money. It never fails. All of them can't say no.

I'm caught up on my work so I take a load over to Toya and come back to get another. When I get back over there, Tom and another guy are standing, talking to two ladies on the other side of where Toya is working. I see this is what they do, stay on the ladies. I'm not mad at them though. They got the gravy ass jobs so they got time to bounce around. Toya says "that's all they do", when she sees me looking over in their direction. I remind her that that's "Her" boy and she was almost caught up. "You not gone ever stop, I see", she says, "No matter what, you not gone let that shit go." "I'm just bullshitting", I say. "But you know he was on your head. And he probably still on your head but he don't know how to play it now." "He told me he still might be on me", she says. "He know me and you talking and I know he don't really care either. That's on him if he make a fool of himself. He used to ask me every day if I wanted lunch then he saw me and you leave out so he stopped asking." "that's crazy", I say. "What guy gone keep trying if they know they not getting anywhere? That's some extra thirsty shit. Some of these motherfuckers act like they ain't never worked with women before. Like the women in here are the only ones in the city. I just don't understand that shit." Sarah is on my mind so I send her a message asking how her day is going and I tell her I miss her. I also tell her I will grab the dinner on my way home. No matter what, she is always going to be first. I will always feel no one will measure up to her. I don't give a damn *who* it is.

The day is winding down and we get a little bit of free time before the bell rings. I get a message from Vickie saying, "have a good day". I reply back "thank you, you do the same." I instantly get another message from her. "So when we gone hang out?" I wasn't even expecting her to come with nothing this so I take a couple seconds before I reply, "when the timing is right, I guess". I'm not trying to start some extra shit on top of the extra shit. My life just not that open to be able to plan shit like that.

Larry is coming down towards me, but saying something that is getting everyone's attention. When I can finally hear him, he is calling a meeting in a small area by the aisle for everyone on the team. He informs us that Don P will no longer be our supervisor as of the end of the day. A couple immediately ask who's next and where is Don P going, but Larry says he doesn't have the answer to that yet. He just knows Don P won't be back after the weekend. That's crazy. Soon as I get used to Don P and his ways, he's gone. Just like that. Larry says it's not uncommon for a supervisor to be moved to another area to help boost quality and see if they can just produce better results from the department. It's just another thing to get used to I guess.

Chapter: Adapt To Change

It's been about three or four months since we got a new supervisor, and everyone is starting to really appreciate the way Don P was. Our new supervisor, Michelle, is totally the opposite of Don P. It's like her attitude is built in or something. Every day is the same with her. She comes in and really doesn't say shit to anyone except when it's work related. I mean, I don't want her to be just talking shit all day, but she can at least speak when she comes by in the morning. The whole mood changes when she comes by.

A lot has changed since I started about seven months ago. The rules are being enforced more now than ever. The headphones are no longer permitted, but you can have your own personal speaker at your work station. I wonder how long it would be before they switch it up and ban those. It would seem like the would rather you have your music playing in your own ear instead of playing it out loud so everyone can hear, but I guess it's the safety issue they are concerned about. Toya is full-time now and she lucked up and ended up on first shift as well. Nothing really has changed with us. Still hanging at lunch time, and even still having a drink after work every now and then. I've been to her place a few times since the first time I went there, too. Her feelings seem like they all over the place now. She tries not to be clingy, but sometimes she can't help herself. I had an idea she would get like this, but she claims she working on it. Jazz tells me that's because I'm probably different than any other guy she's dealt with. It's like Toya sees a different part of things when she's with me. it doesn't matter where we're at, the bar or wherever.

    I see Mack at the truck on break and he says he gotta holler at me about something on the next break. Says he wants to get some input on something. I'm good at the "semi counseling" thing. Maybe one day I'll run for office somewhere. Naw, that political shit not for me. I don't think my attitude will sit well with people. Maybe if I work on my filter, because I pretty much say what's on my mind and worry about the consequences later. Some can deal with it and some can't.

The whole vibe is different now that Don P is gone. It's like a black cloud scene in a movie where the mood is always gloomy and the weather is always rainy. The morale is definitely low right now and people are getting written up at a record pace. I don't know if this was part of a plan to get rid of people or not. It's like everyone knows what's going on with our new supervisor but no one is really doing anything. I take a load over t Toya and ask her what she thinks of the new supervisor. "Wicked bitch from hell" are Toya's exact words. "She must've came back here tripping", I say. "Not really tripping", Toya says," but she came back here and made it known that she in charge. That's just the shit she does, I guess. Every day she says something that remind you that she's in charge. I'm like, bitch you don't have to come by here every day and tell me that you the boss. I already know that. And then they trying to stop us from having a chair at our work station, so she trying to enforce that too. They haven't even said that's it's actually gone happen yet but she already enforcing it. That's the bullshit. A lot of people said they gone switch shifts if she stay around. Shit, she got me intimidated by how she act. I don't be knowing if she having a good day or not, and I don't be trying to spoil it so I don't say shit. She be looking at me crazy and I be looking at her the same way." "Damn, so ya'll catching it back here too", I say. "I guess she the new sheriff and she making that shit happen." "I'll holler at you later", I tell Toya as I head back to my work area.

 Michelle is standing by my work station talking to Larry when I return. She immediately stops talking to him and asks me how long does it take to exchange the bins I take to Toya. "I don't know, about ten minutes", I tell her. "So it take ten minutes to walk right there?", she says, pointing in Toya's direction. I'm almost laughing because I can't even believe she is making a big deal out of it. "Not exactly ten minutes: I say, "but more like seven. What happened, somebody was looking for me or something?" at this point I'm trying to see where this is going. "I was looking for you", Michelle says. "I was walking the line and saw an empty work station so I asked Larry who was working here." "Well, I wasn't really gone", I say. "My job is to take parts over there and that's what I was doing, taking parts." "Ummhmm", she says. "You were working with them girls back there? I don't want you just parading around when you supposed to be working. You have to be around in case I have some questions." "Good morning to you, too", I say. "Good morning", she says. "Now try to stay in your area." She walks off as I stand there confused as what just happened. How can I do my job and stay in my area at the same time? She act like she don't know what the job consists of.

Larry comes back up after Michelle walks off laughing. "I just wanted you to tell her for yourself what your job is. I had told her what you had to do but it wasn't registering or maybe she didn't want it to register, so I figured I'd just let you deal with her. It's like she didn't believe me or had to see for herself. She a different type of breed. Real hands on and somebody got her thinking she untouchable. I hope she know we go through supervisors like the weather changes. She'll learn eventually." "I don't know", i say. "She feeling real bossy."

I can see Mack walking up as the bell is ringing for lunch time. I guess he coming to tell me whatever he was talking about earlier. "What's going on?" I ask as he's walking up. "Man, some bullshit I done got myself into", he says. "I was fucking with this chick from another department, and I already knew she wanted a baby, but I still fucked around with her. Now she pregnant. Out of all the bullshit. So that's where you come in cause' I know you and your girl live together. How the fuck do I tell my girl?" "Wait", I say. "I don't even know if I qualify to give input on that shit. I can relate to living with my girl but that other shit, I can't even relate." Mack is laughing at this point. "For real", I say. "That's some talk show shit, for real. But damn though, she keeping it too? Ya'll ain't even talk about it? I mean, you sound like you already ready to tell." "Shit", Mack says, "when I started fucking around with her she said she couldn't have kids. Well, not have kids but that it was hard for her to get pregnant. She ain't got none right now so I already knew that was gone play a factor in it too. Plus, she was supposedly on birth control. I started messing around with her a little bit after me and my girl started living together and the shit just took off. We definitely wasn't planning on no shit like this, but now this shit done happened, I'm like what the fuck. I already know she keeping it so I don't got no other choice but to tell my girl." "Damn", I say, "that's some helluva shit to drop on her though. How long ya'll been together?" "Three years", Mack said. "I been rocking with the other chick damn near two. I already know, the shit crazy." I guess he could tell by my facial expression that I was thinking the shit sounded crazy. I don't even know where to start really. "Man", I say, "you already know that shit gone blow your household up. And you and your girl ain't got no kids either? That shit gone blow the roof off your house for a minute, really. You probably gone hear about that shit forever. The fucked up part is that you said your girl was talking about she wanted a kid and then you hit her with this. Yeah, that shit gone blow up big time. It's just about how long it's gone be to recover. That shit ain't got no time limit. She might forgive you, but you gone hear about that shit whenever she feel like bringing it up. Not to mention whenever you bring the kid around. I *definitely* can't relate to that." We both start laughing. "Wait before you tell her though. Think about that shit real good. Ain't really no strategy you can come up with. It's all about when you feel like dropping the bomb. Give it four months, fuck it. That way it's halfway through the process and it's not too long before the baby gets here. That's the way I would handle it. If she gone leave, she gone leave before the baby is born, not after. All the emotions and anger might die down once the baby is born, or that shit might skyrocket. I don't know man, she might get pissed every time she see the baby. You gotta keep me posted on that one." "I don't know what I'm gone do, but I'll keep you posted", Mack says as he walks off.

My phone is ringing as I'm walking towards the door to leave out for lunch. It's Vickie saying "hey boo, I'm glad you came in today". "Why is that" I ask. "So I can keep a mental vision in my head of you", she texts back. I'm not even gone touch that shit until later. I need to start paying attention to her really. I don't have time for another crazy chick. If she watching me, that's some stalking shit. I see Michelle as I'm damn near at the door. "Bring me back something if you go to the store." "what you want", I say as I'm walking out the door. "Bring me some chips and something else, whatever you choose." "Ok", I say, as I leave out the door. Why the hell she gotta ask me to bring her some shit? She was just telling me I'm out my area and now she want me to bring her some shit from the store. That's some bullshit, for real.

    Toya is already waiting at my car when I get there. I wasted a few minutes finishing up talking to Mack and Michelle, but I still have time to make a store run. "I saw you talking to Michelle. What that bitch want?" "she wanted me to bring her something back. Ain't that a bitch." "hell naw", Toya says. "That's why I went the other way, just to avoid her ass. She be on some petty shit. Everybody already saying she better keep her distance before she be on flats. These bitches in here ain't bout to let a supervisor just terrorize them with bullshit for no reason." I'm laughing as I pull into the store lot. "You crazy, T. I guess I'll buy the little shit she asked for. Not like it's gone make a difference in the way she acts, but she might act different towards me. maybe redirect her energy elsewhere."

We get back and before I can get out, Toya reaches over and turns my head towards hers and gives me a peck on the lips. I'm not shocked by it, I felt it coming. "And that was for what?", I ask. "That was because I felt like it", she said. "I meant to do it when we first got in the car but you threw me off talking about Michelle. So I waited until we got back. You got a problem with it?" "I just asked a question", I say. "You answered so now I know, you felt like it."

Of course it's a small crowd outside because the weather is warming up, so I know the paparazzi taking notes. As this point I'm sure people have made their own assumptions or whatever, but as long as no one says shit to me and keep the talk to themselves, we good. Be nosy, just from a distance. Karen is outside talking to another female, and of course she makes it known that she sees me by speaking. "What up Mase", she says as we walk past. I speak and keep it moving. I already know that Vickie will get wind of me walking back in with Toya. Maybe, maybe not. Either way, I could care less because Vickie already seen me at the bar with Toya and Jazz so she already know we know each other. Now, if Karen make a story out of it, that's on her.

I can see Michelle a short distance down the line as I walk up to my work area, so I take her stuff to her. She is at the desk, which is located by the side of the line, which a few people can see. I put her stuff on the desk and walk away. "I'm surprised you got it", she says. "I thought you wasn't gone get it." "why would I go through all that and not get it?" I ask. "I don't play games, and I don't waste time. You'll learn that with me." "Well thanks", she says with a smile. "Now you know what snacks I like just in case you feel like getting me something." "Ok", I say as I keep walking. Karen says something as I walk by her and Vickie. I can't really make out what it was but it sound like she said I'm getting brownie points with the supervisor. "I wasn't trying to get points", I say as I turn around. "I 'm trying to keep the bitch off my case. She be on my head so I gotta get her the fuck off. I don't even think she got a good side. Only smirks and attitudes. "They say she act like she like you", Karen says. "Well, she got a crazy way of showing it", I say. Vickie doesn't say anything really, she just has this grin on her face. I guess Karen hasn't told her about earlier yet.

The day goes on and I run into Mack on the way out the door. "Oh well, she keeping it", he said. "But I already felt that shit anyway. Now I just gotta try and hold off telling my girl." "Well, just be prepared for whatever she say", I say. "That's some movie shit but you gotta be prepared for a movie response. If you wait until the baby is here, you *really* gone get the movie! Extra dramatic. But if you want to stay at home and try and figure that shit out, you gotta be ready to deal with the kickback. You might even have to deal with another nigga all in her ear because you leaving her open now. So be prepared if you catch her on some bullshit because you did the ultimate bullshit. You want her to clown though. If she don't clown, you then you gotta watch for all type of bullshit." "I already know", Mack says. "Shit, I'm still trying to figure out if I can deal with hearing the bullshit every day. She might dip! It might be too much for her to deal with." "Just sit down and kick it with her", I say. "Eventually, you have to tell her." We splitting up towards our cars by this time so I crack a little smile and tell Mack, "you on some straight up VH1 shit right now. Let me know how that shit go." That's some crazy shit. Extra stressful shit that I definitely don't want to ever relate to.

I'm getting myself situated and hear my phone going off. It's Vickie, sending me a text message asking why I leave without saying bye. I call her to save some time. "So, what's up", she says as she answers the phone. She doesn't even say hello. "You just gone leave without giving me a hug or nothing?" Surprised, I don't even really know what to say. "I mean, I didn't know you wanted to see me before you left. I actually thought you leave out with Karen." "Most times I do", she says. "Today I wanted to see you though. You still close?" I take a few seconds before I answer because this shit threw me off. "I'm just pulling out the parking lot. You must still be around here?" "At the gas station but you can meet me around the corner from it." "Call me when you park", I tell her as I hang up the phone. I already know she at the hot gas station that a lot of people go to after work. I wasn't going up there anyway. She was thinking the same thing too, that's probably why she picked that side street. After a couple minutes, she calls and lets me know where she is. I pull up a short time later, but I don't even know what kind of car she's in so I slow roll down the street until I see her roll down her window. Her windows so damn dark I wouldn't've noticed her if she didn't roll the window down. I must say, Vickie is definitely riding good. I park behind her as she gets out. "You riding good I see", I tell her as I walk up to her. "Well, when I first started, my dad got a brand new car so he gave me this and told me I just have to finish the payments. It ain't like it's new, it's a couple years old." "Whatever", I say. "You riding a Lexus, so that just ain't normal. Even if pops did give it to you, you still riding extra good. So , what he cop since he gave this to you?" "A new Lexus", she says laughing. "He said he love the way their cars ride and durability so he sticking with them for a while. He had this first and now he got the new GS. I'm not mad at him though. I'll glady take his little hand me downs. This car is only 5 years old, but the miles so low because he didn't even drive it that much. Even when he went out of town he rented a car. It's crazy because it's still under warranty. Long as I don't have to worry about that, I'm good." "He not about to let his baby girl be on the side of the road anyway", I say. "So you know before he gave it to you he knew it wasn't gone be any problems with it. So you just stay solo huh", I ask. "Yep, just me and my apartment. No kids, so I just kick back. No dude either. That's been for almost a year. Maybe over a year. I just finished school so I'm waiting to see if I want to do the supervisor thing here or somewhere else. I might go into HR too. See, this is what the last guy couldn't deal with, my schedule. I was working full-time and going to school full-time but I was on a mission. He didn't see that mission, he saw them other bitches in his face telling him what he needed. So he had a little talk with me and we went our separate ways. No hard feelings. He even calls me every now and then. Sometimes I answer, sometimes I don't. I don't stay where I used to so he doesn't know where I stay or nothing like that. So you don't have to worry about him popping up at my place." I interrupt immediately. "So I'm gone be at your place?" Vickie starts laughing. "Come give me a hug so you can be on your way. And let me know when we gone have our after-work drink." "Ok", I say as I hug her and head back to my car. "I'll figure it out."

Damn, Vickie is definitely a different type of female. I can see why she acts the way she does, though. That's probably all she know. I can tell from her little mini story that she grew up spoiled as hell but that's not her fault. Pops must've kept her laced up so she extra independent. That's a good thing though. She a little bit more laid back than Toya, but they both got their shit together. But, bad timing for both of them.

I run into a traffic jam on the way home and instantly blame Vickie. Shit like this is like a sign. If I would've just left, instead of meeting up with her, I would be pass this already. Bullshit like this is why I don't fuck around. It's always something to throw it off. We got a couple days off for the holiday coming up so me and Sarah got a little getaway planned. It's good every now and then to just get away from everything and everyone. You need life refreshers like that to stay sane. It also helps when you have someone to take these with.

Chapter: Changes

It's coming up to my one-year anniversary, which means my yearly raise. That's another benefit of being full-time. You get that raise every year. That year went by fast too. At least it seemed like it did. I guess I'm officially bred in now. I didn't write my life script up like this, but it is what it is. It's a lot of people that complain at work, but it's not too many people quitting. And it's definitely more people trying to get in than trying to leave out them doors. I hear a lot of people saying they hate they job but they still walk through them doors every day to get that money. Prime example is TJ. Every time I talk to him, he got a injury. If it's not his migraines, it's something else. And he swear everybody always hating on him. After ten minutes of talking to him, I be feeling like I need a shrink. Like damn, you done gave me a damn headache by listening to the bullshit. Then it's Kamesha. She probably worse than TJ. She got every condition he has, except she is more dramatic/ she's a floater but she works near my area sometimes. Not a day goes by that she doesn't go to medical. She can work on a job for damn near the whole day and still somehow feel the need to go to medical. It's like a light comes on in her head like "Oh, shit, you haven't been to medical today", and before you know it, she gone. And if it's a tedious job, she definitely not lasting for the whole day. Her carpal tunnel will kick in. you know it's bad when people expect you to go to medical and be shocked when you don't. But, that's a way of life for some people. I guess they need that attention or whatever sympathy they get.

    Michelle hasn't changed one bit since the first day she hit the building. Shit, really it's like she getting worse than she was before. She barely even speak, well she pick and choose who she wants to talk to. That shit crazy. When it's time to talk about the job though, she the first to open her mouth. She don't ever speak unless it's job shit. Like she programmed or some shit. Who the fuck is training these people? They would be better off managers at fast food or in a retail store, than up in here. How does she expect to get anything done hen she has this attitude and barely speak? Respect is earned not given. And the way she acting now, she damn near done fucked up with everybody. It's only about a handful of people that actually like her. Some of them probably just intimidated by her so they ass kiss. I refuse to do that shit and I guess that's why we clash so much. Not every day, but we do have our run ins where we both feel strong about our views on some things. She gives me my respect though, and I give her hers. I still feel she's a bitch for no reason sometimes, and I'm sure she knows it. A couple of co-workers already told me she think I think she's the biggest bitch. That right there is evidence that she knows she acting like a bitch but choose to be that way. I don't need a reminder every day to let me know who the damn boss is. I already know that shit.

    Once you get a full year in, you get another sense of relief. The first comes after you are officially full-time and the next is when you have your one-year anniversary. That solidifies your seniority. Seniority is the way of pulling rank in the plant. If you want to make any moves as for shift preference, job preference, and even leaving early, your seniority might play a factor. The longer you have been employed equals the length of leeway you have. If you only have two months of seniority you damn sho don't have the same pull as someone with two years seniority. Experience is key but years are a must!

With my one-year anniversary, I know from what Mack told me that every one after that flies by. I still have to ask him about his little situation. It's probably really out of control by now. That shit is something I never want to go through, for real.

When I first started I had noticed that a lot of people rocked their kicks to work. Expecially the Jordans. You can find J's everywhere in the plant, from guys to females, even the bosses be rocking them. Even when a new pair come out, somebody gone rock them to work, no matter what type of job they have. Yes, they might fuck them up at work, but that's another issue they'll worry about later. That's that fashion shit that people told me about. Some people have to make a fashion statement every day. It's not uncommon to see people looking like they not going to work and they at work. You might even see a couple Louie bags on some shoulders. Yeah, it be like that sometime.

I'm not gym shoe crazy like these youngins these days, buy I do have a few pair that I can bring out. Since my seniority date just passed, I picked today as the day to wear a pair of my retro Jordans. They not coming out anytime soon so I know some people gone have some "what the fuck" faces when they notice them. I can already see a few heads turning as I get my area together. Vickie comes up and gives me a hug before she goes down to her area. "I see you got your Jordans on, you trying to be like me", she says as she walks away. When I check her feet I notice she has on a pair of retros too. With her spoiled ass. Then I notice her ass, and her walk, so I send her a text message telling her I like her walk. "How my ass look?" is her response. She caught me off guard with that one but since she opened the door, I respond with "I guess it look all right but I need a closeup. I can't really tell through that uniform." I don't know if that's a way to reel people in or what, but it's like the women already know guys looking, so that's like the first thing they care about, how they look. Same shit Toya asked. How her ass look. Shit, that shit really not that easy to tell through no jumpsuit, so I'm really telling the truth when I say I need a closeup. I can see the shape but that's it. It's the outside clothes that count. Vickie replies back "I'll ask you again after work." After thinking about it, I reply back "ok". I guess she wore some jeans or something that she want me to see her in. I can be a judge in that category for her. Now she gone have me looking at her all day, trying to see if I can see something.

The bell rings but I haven't seen Toya today yet. I guess she might've came in and went straight to her work station. I know she hasn't called in because she doesn't have enough time for that yet. I'll stop over there at the first break and see if she at work.

Larry comes down and says he might be leaving to go to another department. Damn, it's changes all around this place now. I ask Larry does he know who will be taking his place and he says not yet but he'll let me know before he leaves. The good thing is that we will get to meet our new TL before he gets to the area. As least we will get to see what type of person we will be dealing with and what to expect. It took some time to get used to Larry, but I have to admit that Larry showed me everything I know about the area and the jobs in the area. When I first started he had a difficult way of handling things, but over time he got used to how I was and I got used to his ways. He didn't really give out bathroom breaks until I came here, and even the other workers noticed that. It's like he had a different outlook on his role and duties. You could tell the team was appreciating him more, which in turn made his days easier.

    The bell rings and I make my way over towards Toya. When I get over there, Jazz is already there, flapping. She don't even realize how much she runs her mouth. If it's any business or gossip in the plant, Jazz gone know about it, or be one call away from finding about it. She like the breaking story news reporter. Extra nosy. When Toya sees me, she immediately stops paying attention to Jazz and comes up and hugs me. "Goodmorning boo", she says. "You all right?" I ask. "Yes, I'm good now", she says. "Ok, well go ahead and finish running your mouth", i say. "I was just making sure you were here." "Of course I'm here", she says. "I just got my raise, I ain't trying to go backwards." "Right", I say as I'm walking away. I see they had their little McDonalds sandwiches. I ain't even feel like putting them on blast though. Matter of fact, I *am* gone put them on blast because I buy them shit all the time. They could've at least got me a hash brown, anything! When I get back to my area and put the empty bins down, I send Toya a message. "So who stopped at McDonalds and didn't get me nothing?" I guess she was trying to get her words together because it took a few minutes before she replied. Even when she did, she didn't answer the question but just sent back she didn't get the food. Okay, so I guess Jazz bought the food. I reply back that she could've told Jazz to get me something too. She then sends back that Jazz didn't buy it either so I already know some dude got it. Ok, I'm done with it then. I'm not about to play detective over some bullshit food.

Larry is standing, talking to another guy when I get by my work station. He introduces the guy as Ced, and says he will be our next TL. From the looks of it, it doesn't look like Ced is ready to work at all. He has on a du-rag, and has his brush in his hands the whole time, like he can't wait to brush his hair. Another quick glance reveals his semi-new gym shoes and his non-work outfit. I just think to myself, aww shit, I hope he not a lazy motherfucker. Larry wasn't just lazy, but he needed to be molded into a decent TL. It's looking like we gone have to mold the new guy too. He looks kind of young and like his father or somebody got him in here, if you know what I mean. "You got some big shoes to fill", I tell Ced as he is looking over the work area. "I heard", he says. "I'm just trying to keep up whatever process Larry had going on and keep everything smooth within the team. Not trying to change nothing ya'll got going already." I can tell by his attitude that he doesn't want no trouble. He just want to come in here, do his little job, and wear his street clothes. He says he been a TL for three years and he came to this department from assembly at SHAP, Sterling Heights

Assembly Plant. He says he came from an area that had the hardest jobs on the line, so this shit shouldn't be nothing to him. I can see the curious looks on everyone's faces while they watch Larry show Ced the ropes. Of course, until he actually takes over, Ced will be the perfect TL, but it's what he does after the training that matters. Larry never really did say what he was going to do next, either , the more I think about it. I gotta ask him to see where he going. Usually, when people leave an area for another area it's for an upgrade. I can't see anyone leaving to go to another area to do harder work.

    Larry leaves Ced to work on the job with the regular person, and when I see him walk away, I call him over to where I am. "So, what you think?", I ask him. "I think ya'll gone be all right", he says. "He came from the Trim department so I know for sure they have the hardest jobs around. This shit over here should be a cakewalk. You see how he dressed though, so don't let him just be clean all day. Since he didn't want to get his jumpsuit today, let him get a little dirty. At least he don't seem lazy. I'm trying to get him on the jobs so he can know a few of them before I go. I got one week left so he got enough time to know everything, at least the important stuff."

After listening to Larry, I feel a little more comfortable about the situation. Plus, Larry gone be working with him a few more days so he will get to see some spur of the moment type shit. "So, you going to another department or you switching shifts? What's up?" "Actually, I'm going out to have surgery. I been putting it off for a while so I finally decided to have it." "Some major shit or some routine shit?" I ask. "Not routine, but not really major, either", he says. "They said the last time I was there that it was something they wanted to take out but that it could wait. I'm just trying to get back. That sixty-five percent you get for being out is bullshit. I need all mines." "I feel you on that", I say. "I guess since the job not at fault they don't want to pay. That's the bullshit but I guess that's the process." Larry jumps right in after I stop talking. "Crazy part is my doctor said the job might have had something to do with it, but he just can't be sure. See, the air and certain chemicals just linger because of the lack of airflow. He said it's possible that I could have gotten it from being in certain areas for long periods of time, he just can't pinpoint it. And then I used to smoke so that's playing a factor too. Long as they catch it early, he said I should be good." "So it's like some Cancer shit then", I say. "Damn, man, you be calm as hell with *that* shit on your brain? But I guess it's all out your hands so you just keep it locked in. that's some helluva shit right there. I'm gone pray for you though. You gone be smooth." "I'm not even really worried", he says. "I just don't want to fall behind too much on my priorities and shit. That's two months of waiting, and hopefully they send my money on time. I've heard of people waiting damn near a month before they got their first check. That's fucked up. The good part in all this is I don't have no kids so it's just me and I should be able to stay afloat." I nod my head in agreeance as he walks off. Damn, he on a bad mission. Sound like he almost got throat Cancer and they trying to catch it. I wonder has he told anyone else besides me, or do they think he going out on medical for something else. It's not my place to tell but that's some serious shit. I hope it all works out.

Shit like Larry's case usually make you wonder. It's not something you hear about all the time, but it may be possible that the air in here is fucked up. If it's not a mass population thing no one will ever really look into it. As long as it's isolated cases or a low number, it will be looked at as a personal issue and not a company issue. Of course the company doesn't want to claim responsibility, so they not gone just put some information out there and then be dealing with lawsuits from everywhere.

That long talk with Larry put me kind of behind on my work so I have to rush to catch up on it. Toya must be good though, because she hasn't came over here asking what's up with the parts or nothing. She probably back there running her mouth anyway. We got a little time before lunch so I can get ahead by then and be caught up for the rest of the day.

When I get back to her area, Toya is running her mouth as usual. Her buddy Tom is keeping her company, to no surprise. Some things you just can't control, and whatever they got going is one of them. Not trying to interrupt, I drop off the parts and head back to my area. Toya doesn't say anything and of course Tom doesn't either. She can never say shit to me about speaking to anyone. She probably have more convo with him than any convo I have with any female. I can bet that because I usually don't talk much in here. I try to have my music going and stay in my zone. I only watch out for the supervisor, and that's only to make sure I don't get caught with my headphones on. With the way I see some of these dudes all up in females faces, I can't be like that anyway. Camping out at a chick work station just ain't my style. That's too much attention for me, but I guess it doesn't matter for some people because I see it all the time. Usually the woman is working and the guy is standing to the side, talking, while she working. Not my style. Plus I don't have that type of time on my hands, or that much shit to say at work anyway.

I get back to my area and the line is down. Vickie is talking to the young lady that works a few stations down from me. She pretty much wraps up her conversation when she sees me at my work station and walks down where I'm at. "Don't be looking shocked because I stopped down here", she says, in her proper voice. "I'm definitely not shocked", I say. "I knew you was gone stop by here, especially if I'm right here. You not just gone be down here by me without stopping right here. We both know that." Vickie is smiling at this point. "You think you know me huh", she says. "You don't know if I was gone stop or not. I could've walked right past and didn't say nothing, or I could've walked on the other side." "But you didn't", I say. "You did exactly what you should've did, stop by here. You know you wasn't going to be down by me and not even stop and say nothing. Even if it was a quick visit, you still gotta stop." "Listen to you", she says. "You act like you know me or something. You don't know me." "Whatever", I say as she walks off down towards her work station. Vickie cold, but her style make her colder. Her attitude just tops it off. She would probably be the only one that I would deal with on a serious level if I already didn't have a situation. Toya cool, but Vickie, that's something different. Speaking of Toya, I haven't heard anything from her about lunch so I guess she doing her own thing. She hasn't said shit about what's going on.

The bell rings and I make my way towards the door. Since I haven't heard from Toya I walk at a slower pace than usual, just in case she sees me walking out. As I'm passing the bathrooms on the way out, Vickie and Karen are coming out. "Where we going?", Vickie asks in a nosy way. "To hit a couple blocks", I say. "You riding with me?" "Yeah, I'll go", she says, not even thinking twice. She then asks Karen to grab her something off the truck and gives her some money. "I guess I'll see you back at the line", she tells Karen. "But if I'm not back on time, call the police", she says laughing. "If I kidnap you, you gone be glad", I say as we walk out the door.

We get outside to my car and I still haven't heard anything from Toya. No way she'll be able to place the blame on me. I even waited extra time just in case she came out late. So that's on her now. I pull out the parking lot and head on my way. "So this what you do at lunch?", Vickie asks. "Yes", I say. "I hit the store too though and ride the neighborhood. Nothing spectacular." "Ummhmm", she says. "I really don't go out at lunch. I just stay in my area pretty much and just relax until the bell rings. It feels good to get out and get some fresh air though. It be feeling like jail up in there sometimes. I can see why you get out every day. " "It keeps me level headed", I say as we pull in the store parking lot. "Light or dark", I ask her before I get out. "What you mean?", she asks. "I'm about to get me a shot, you want one?", I ask. Vickie is laughing now. "Boy, get me two. One shot ain't gone do that much for me. I need at least a double. Not saying I'm a lush, but if I'm gone sip something, I need to be able to be in my zone. Get dark." I go in and grab two shots of dark and some gum. Gotta be prepared for nosy ass Michelle, in case she wanna be all up in my face . we down the shots as I pull off and head back to the job. The weather is nice out so of course you have those who chill outside at lunch sitting around at tables. Plus, the groups of people that are just standing around, chilling. I already knew this was a possibility when I left out with Vickie. It's always a few people hanging around outside when the weather is nice, so it's nothing new. As I'm pulling into the aisle to park, I think I notice Jazz walking towards the door to go in. it doesn't look like Toya is with her either. Surprised at that, but I'm sure Toya didn't miss riding with me. usually she'll text me or something, talking shit if I leave her. Not today. She hasn't said shit since I saw her talking with Tom earlier. Mack is walking in at the same time as me and he gives me this surprised look when he sees who I'm with. I can tell without even saying anything, just by his facial expression. We both nod and keep it moving.

Just when I though I had made it back in without being spotted, I see Jazz walking towards my direction. It's pretty much nothing I can do at this point but speak, except Jazz already on top of it. "What's up Mase", she says in a sarcastic tone. I can tell by the way she said it that in her mind she was saying "yeah, I see you". the look on her face was priceless. Of course she didn't say shit to Vickie, and Vickie didn't say shit to her either. I guess they only speak to each other when they drinking.

We get to my area and I stop and put my things down and Vickie keeps walking to her area. A few people definitely noticed us walking up the line together and I'm still getting glances as I get ready. It's not that I was just walking with one of the most hated females in here, it's the fact that most of the whole work area saw it. Not to mention the few guys that probably tried to talk to her. Maybe that's why they looking, trying to figure out what kind of game I had to use on her. Little do they know, I didn't use any. She chose me. I'm just being myself. You don't have to go overboard to get the girl. Vibe with who vibe with you, that's my mentality. I'm more of an observer than a big talker, so I gotta feel the vibe before I just jump out there. Vickie gave the first vibe and I went with the vibe. You can pursue a woman, but you have to be able to read the signs to know your next action. So far, I'm reading the shit out of the signs.

No word yet from Toya, even after the whole lunch thing and running into Jazz. Now that's interesting. I know Jazz already done told Toya that she saw me, but Toya hasn't sent a message or nothing, which is the surprise. I guess she gone wait until she sees me face to face. I really don't want to hear no bullshit anyway though because she did that to herself.

I'm caught upon my work so now I can take a couple bins over to Toya. Michelle is walking up the line so I try to hurry and be gone before she gets down by me but she catches me before I can get out of sight. "So how long that's gone take?", she asks. I already see where this is going but I'm not about to just make it easy for her. She ain't even speak today, but she want to talk about the job? Nope. "How long what's gone take?", I ask. "For me to take the parts over there?" "Yeah", she says. "I don't know", I reply. "You wanna come with me to time me , or you wanna take them over there yourself so you can see? I don't put a time limit on this job, I just do the job and let time take care of itself." I can tell she is getting a little attitude by the look on her face, but I feel like she didn't even have to say shit because it's not that serious. "You see how you just got smart", she says. "I asked you a simple question and you went all off, talking about some other shit." I can see the few people in my area starting to pay attention because it's not like we whispering, but we not just yelling either. Let me dead the situation. "You asked me how long it's gone take like you were getting at something though. Like you was gone time me or something and that's why I said what I said. I wasn't getting smart, I just answered your question. It probably wasn't the answer you wanted, that was the problem. But you making me late now, so you gone help me take this shit over here or you gone wait until I get back?" it's a couple people snickering and giggling because of the way I'm talking to her, because they know she is a bitch at times, but she not just gone come at me with bullshit. After waiting a couple of seconds she says, "I'll see you when you get back over here".

I get over to Toya area and Jazz is back there so I already know she told Toya whatever story she wanted to. It's not like Jazz asked me anything, so I can just assume she said whatever she wanted. They both get quiet when I walk up. "Ya'll ain't gotta stop talking because I walked up", I say. "I already know ya'll be running your mouths so ain't no way ya'll back here quiet. And what happened to you earlier?", I ask Toya. "I didn't hear from you so I stayed in", she says. "I waited on a call or something, and after I didn't hear from you, I just said oh well." It sound like she putting the blame on me right now. "So your phone was broke?" I ask. "Any other time you use your phone when you want something, what happened today? When I came over here earlier you had company so I kept it moving. I did think you would contact me before lunch though, seeing that you were busy when I came back there. I guess ya boy Tom threw yo mind off, that's why you stayed in for lunch. "Really?", Toya says. "That's how you gone act? I mean, yeah, he was over here but you still could've said something." "Look", I say interrupting her, "if you wanted to ride out, you would've said something. The whole damn morning went by and you didn't even mention it. C'mon now. Then you try and put the blame on me? When you were the one busy. Hell naw, I can't take the blame for that one. I did everything I usually do, but *you* switched it up." Now I can tell by her attitude that she switching to defense mod. She pauses, looks at Jazz, then asks, "so that's why you had that bitch in the car? You already know I know so don't even bullshit me." Without hesitation, I say, "It had a little to do with it, but you ain't say shit all morning. I came back here earlier and you were talking. You didn't stop talking or say hold up or nothing. So apparently your conversation was extra deep so you didn't want to stop it. I figured you would at least send me a message but you didn't. so after the whole morning went by, it wasn't no way I was about to check and see if you were rolling with me at lunch. Shit, when I checked on you, you were good! I already told you, I'm not about to be standing around, waiting on you to finish your conversations. You already know that. I do a quick glance at the time on her computer. Now I gotta get back over here before Michelle start looking for me. I guess we'll finish this later." "Yes, we definitely gone finish this later", she says.

    I don't know what the fuck Toya expect out of me but I'm not the one. Whoever she used to deal with or whatever got her head fucked up. Or maybe it's the dudes in here, I don't know. I *do* know that she gone do this on my wavelength or not at all. And if she really like the guy she should just say that shit. No need to hide it.

Michelle is standing by my work station when I return. "You had to go see your girlfriend?", she asks. I'm tripping because first Toya not my girlfriend, and second, I can't even believe Michelle even spending that much time paying attention. Damn, all the employees she over and she seem to be paying attention to what I'm doing the most. "Well, that's not my girlfriend", I say. "You know I have to go over there to drop off her parts. That's part of my job. I can't avoid going over there." "Whatever", she says. "I heard you got a little girlfriend back there. You know people talk, right? I can't remember where I was, but somebody saw you coming from back there and said you were talking to your girlfriend." "Damn, people snitching on me now? They don't even know what's going on but have so much to say. People nosy than a motherfucker. They make something out of nothing." "Well, they your co-workers", she says. Michelle walks off and I start to look around to see if I can see the snitch on someone's face. Still shocked that somebody feel the need to tell on me like that, but whatever. I heard about this bullshit when I first started though. Some people be more interested in everybody else's business than they are with their own.

The break is coming up so I get ready to take a load of parts to Toya. Vickie sends me a message asking what I have to do after work. I know I'm supposed to chat with Toya but that shit shouldn't take but five to ten minutes. I send Vickie a text saying I got about thirty minutes to chill after work. Toya just want to vent about everything, so I'm gone hear her out and that's pretty much it. She on bullshit herself, but I guess since Jazz told her she saw me, she got something to say. I'm already prepared to hear the bullshit.

The break comes and I see Mack while I'm on my way to the vending machine. "So what happened with the baby situation?", I ask. "Shit, my girl left for about a week after the baby was born but she back now. I couldn't really trip too bad because all the shit was my fault, so I ain't really say shit. She just started staying there when I have the baby over. She used to leave and stay at her mothers' whenever I had my daughter, but she loosened up a bit." "That shit crazy", I say. "I already know you damn near crazy dealing with it. One day she good and the next, she on some terrorizing shit. You probably don't even know what to expect." "Man", he says, "I'm just hoping the jekyl and hyde shit eventually wears off.

On my way back I get a message from Toya saying, "I need to talk after work. Thirty minutes?" I guess that's what she was referring to earlier when she said she'll talk to me later. She really could say everything she had to say while we here but I'll hear her out I guess. I send her a reply "I guess". At this point I already got my mind made up. I gotta tell Vickie we have to do a raincheck for another day. Probably would have rather saw her anyway after work, but I'll wait until next time. I want to be sitting down somewhere and not clock watching when I hang with Vickie. I send Vickie a message saying I have to take a raincheck and she replies back, "Ok, but I still want my hug after work". Damn, she still wanna see me. It ain't shit but a hug so it won't throw my time off with Toya. I just have to make it short and quick so I don't lose track of time.

Ced is settling in pretty good with everyone on the team, which is a great thing and somewhat surprising. Not really surprising but when you have to go from one atmosphere to another, it can be challenging. Not to mention dealing with different attitudes on a daily basis. It's all about knowing who you work with really. Being a TL is as easy as you make it. If you have a team that's all for you, you good. If you get a team that isn't, your days can be hell. I've noticed that people only want to get off the line once in the morning and once in the afternoon. That would be the easiest thing to do if I was the TL, give a break. If that's going to help my day go smoother by giving out a break, then so be it. I will never understand why people won't give out a break to make their job easier. I guess Larry getting used to being at home kicking his feet up. I think he said he'll be out for a couple weeks the come back and be in his new position. I gotta find out where he's working nd go holler at him.

The day is winding down so I I prepare my last bin of parts to take to Toya. I already know what the discussion is going to be about so I really don't see a point in speaking on it. It's not going to change my way of thinking. When I get over there I'm reminded of the reason I ct the way I do. Tom is walking away as I'm walking up. I don't even say nothing, I just drop off the parts and proceed to head back so I can get ready to leave. I get a message from Toya saying to meet up at Pauline's. that's cool. Not too far and it won't throw my ride home off.

The bell rings and I head towards the door. Vickie is walking with Karen and immediately slows down so I can catch up to her. "You gone walk me to my car?", she asks. "I mean, I guess I'm obligated to now", I say with a grin. "You waited on me." I can tell Vickie is totally different than most of the women in here. That's probably the reason so many people think she stuck up or whatever. She only fuck with a certain amount of people, she does her job, and leaves. Nothing extra. I guess some people don't understand that.

We get to her car and I give her a hug before she gets in. with it being the end of the day, I know it was all eyes on us as we walked across the parking lot. She tells me to text her or something if I get the chance as I walk away towards my car. The perfect chick but not the perfect situation, is what I think to myself. I get in my and sit for a couple seconds and just process my day and everything that went on. Michelle is turning out to be something else, Toya turning into Ms. Extra Friendly, and Vickie is opening up more and more as time goes on. Well, let me get over to this bar so I can hear this bullshit.

When I get up to the bar, Toya is already there, sitting in her car. Before I can park, she pulls up alongside of me and says we can go to the park and talk. "Fine with me, I'll follow you', I tell her as we both pull off. I guess she just wanted to get me away from the job and used the bar as a meeting spot. The park not too far away from here though, so it's no big deal. It should be pretty empty out there too, because most people only be out there on the weekends.

The park is empty, just as I thought when we get there. She pulls up and I tell her to go to the other side, out of view of pretty much everything. I came down to this part a few times with Mack and JP when they were smoking. I tell Toya I'll come to her car so she doesn't have to get out. By the time I park and get to her car, she has already climbed to her backseat through the front. She only five feet six so that wasn't shit to do. I got a confused look on my face and she can tell, so she says "just get in" when I look at her. "So", she says, as she lifts a blunt, "let's clear the air". "I already told you that ain't shit going on with me and Tom. Yeah, he likes me, and even brought me and Jazz breakfast that time you were wondering, but I don't like him like that. He already know me and you talking or whatever, but he doesn't really care. Why, I don't know, but that's how he act. And to top it off, the motherfucker married! On top of all the bullshit he be doing, not even talking about me, but the shit I see him doing with other bitches. And he tells me he married. That's why he was over there so much today, trying to explain his situation. It's crazy because I don't know how he thought I would just give in, especially after he just ran off his whole resume'. Jazz said a lot of females wouldn't give a shit, so that's why he didn't feel it was no big deal telling me. I mean, I'm cold-hearted but not that cold. As much bullshit he be talking, all up in people faces. He is the last person I thought would be married." I'm tripping right now because a part of me is like wow, and another part wants to laugh. I think I'm just as shocked as Toya. The way Tom acts says nothing towards him being married. As many chicks I see him talking to, that's the last thing I would've expected. "That's the bomb for the day", I say. "I guess you learn something new every day."

Toya quickly shifts the conversation after a few seconds. "And you know I know you were hanging with that bitch at lunch time. You already knew Jazz was gone tell me that shit. So I guess that's why you didn't text me at lunch, because you knew you were hanging with her ass." "That's not really the case", I say. "You sitting here like you the victim and your own actions were the reason for most of the bullshit. When I came over there earlier, you just kept talking to Tom. You already know I'm not gone stop and interrupt you, so that's why I just left. I'm not a hater or a blocker. Whatever you and Tom got going on, that's on you. You might not be trying to fuck with him but you definitely like his conversation." Toya quickly interrupts, "just like you and Vickie huh?" "We not talking about me right now", I say. "I'm trying to find out what's going on and you keep re-directing the questions. But since you keep asking, I didn't plan on going out with Vickie. She was right there when I was going out the door and I hadn't heard from you so I said yeah, she could go. She had perfect timing. You didn't say shit about lunch or nothing. I figured you had other plans. When something points to bullshit, I'm gone think the bullshit, especially if that's all I can go on."

After hearing me explain to her what really happened and the reason for my actions, Toya said "okay, now I have to worry about the bitch Vickie, I guess. I should've known something was up when she brought you that drink. Jazz told me that shit too. And now the bitch all up in your car." All I can do is just listen because I feel like Toya brought the shit on herself. She is quiet for a few seconds, then she says "well, this shit done worked my nerves up now and I think you gone have to give me some before you leave."

I'm outdone by everything she just said, but I guess she got turned on by the shit. She already started taking down her pants without me saying anything. Before I know it, she got her hands in my pants, and then, next, she is sitting on my lap. Her windows are tinted so it's not like anyone could see us. Plus the park was empty, so that was the last thing to worry about. After it was over, Toya just sat on my lap with her eyes closed, shaking her head. "I needed that", she says. "I think that was my problem. I just needed to see you. Sorry if I was tripping, but my hormones were all over the place and I needed to see you. I know the bitch on your head now so I gotta be a step ahead of her, too." I'm still trying to process everything that just went on. My mind is everywhere right now. I get out, give her a peck on the lips, and head over to my car to get ready for this drive home.

Chapter: Tragedy

Over the next few months I kept an extra low profile when it came to the ladies at work. Ced had settled all the way in as our new TL and things were going pretty smooth, until we learned that

Larry had to have surgery. It took us a couple of days until we learned that it was to remove a cancerous tumor. Yes, it can be a simple procedure but it also has its side effects. Larry had planned on being out for only about two weeks, but I had heard from some people the he had complications from the surgery and he had to be out longer. Of course we had our little disagreement in the beginning, but Larry was one of the best TL's on the floor I heard.

  Mack had known Larry since he started at the job, so they used to hang out every now and then and maybe hit a bar or two. They weren't the closest of friends but they still hung out every once in a while. I see Mack when I'm coming in the door one day and I can tell by his plain face and whole demeanor that something was out of the ordinary. He's just standing there shaking his head at me as I walk through the door. I can tell something is wrong so I ask him "what's up"? when he started speaking, it was as if he was speaking in slow motion, or maybe I was just hearing it in slow motion. "Man", he said, "Larry died last night. JP called and told me at like three this morning. It was a shock so I went to his Facebook page and his sister had posted it up on Larry page. That shit crazy man because somebody had just told me he was leaving the hospital tomorrow and then JP called and told me that shit." I'm standing there in silence, shocked at what Mack just told me. It's also early as hell so the shit hasn't all the way processed, but this shit doesn't seem real. "Damn", I say, "that's fucked up. That shit was *that* bad. I had heard he had complications but I didn't know it was that serious. that's crazy." "Unbelievable", Mack says. "I knew something was wrong when I saw JP name popping up at three on my phone. I guess they hadn't heard from him so they went over there and saw his car in the driveway. After they knocked on the door, they called the police and they got in and found him laying on the couch. He didn't say nothing else, he just told me he would keep me posted." "Well, keep me posted on whatever", I say.

    Walking in today felt different than any other day at work. When I get towards my work area, I can see people huddled up in small groups. They probably talking about the same news that I just heard, I assume. The mood is one I'll never forget. Larry had been with the company for a few years and had been well-liked by many. You can tell that work is the last thing on peoples' minds.

Michelle is walking the line as she usually does, not even acknowledging that a co-worker has passed. I thought it would be some type of moment of silence or something at least to show some type of recognition for a former employee. I even asked Michelle did she hear about it and she said someone spoke to her briefly about it this morning, but that was it. Damn, I see they really don't give a shit if you in good health or not. They only want your services to make vehicles, and today it really shows.

The first bell rings and the day starts just as any other day, you can tell that people are wondering if they are going to release some more information or not on Larry. I can see our steward Paul walking the line speaking to people as they work. He comes up to me and asks if I'm good. I tell him yeah, but they could've at least acknowledged Larry or something this morning. He says he doesn't know for sure but they might do something later on today. What good is that shit? Whatever they planned on saying later, they can say now. Paul says they have grievance counselors available but he will have to get back with us on how to handle it. It's plain and clear that a lot of people are disturbed by what happened, I don't see the reason to wait.

I get my first two loads together and take them over to Toya. She is just as shocked as I am about Larry. He was the first to show us the ropes. Even though he used to be on some bullshit, he still managed to loosen up and become a better team player. Everyone says the new hires were the ones who got him into helping out more and not just training people for ten minutes and them leaving them. All this shit is just a shock. That's life though. Gotta make the best of it.

You can tell by the vibe that everyone is just trying to get the day over with and just go home. We already feel like they disrespected Larry by not even mentioning him, and then our reps didn't enforce anything, so everyone just ready to leave at this point. I understand the company is all about business, but I thought the Union would make something happen.

Lunch time is approaching and today, I'm definitely having me a shot. After everything that's went on, I might have two. I get a text from Toya saying not to leave her. She already know not to be bullshitting, especially today. I want every minute of my time today. They lucky they don't give us a hour. I'll hit up Pauline's.

I see the medical cart riding pass as I'm getting ready to leave out. I see it turn the corner down by the end of the line, but I can still see the flashing lights on the wall. I can't even think about who works down there before someone walking by says," that bitch Kainesha on her bullshit again". I guess she having another dramatic episode, or she got another injury. If she need the cart then ain't no telling, it might be something new. Oh well, there go the bell. I guess I'll hear about that shit later. On my way to the door I hear a few random voices mentioning Larry. I guess he was well-known throughout the plant.

I get to my car and wait for Toya to walk up. She probably feels like she is damn near my girl at this point. It's been over a year so I'm pretty sure she has some type of mental title on it. I'm sure a few people probably thinking whatever to themselves, but that's all their doing, saying it to themselves.

Toya gets in and the first thing she says is, "this shit feel like a dream. I know he wasn't family or nothing, but this shit definitely makes you feel some type of way. When you work with someone damn near two years, it's like you get used to seeing them. I'm sure we would've still seen Larry, even though he was going to another department. I mean, we be here more than we be at home so it's like this our own little family." "I know", I say, as I pull into the store parking lot. 'Well, we gone put this drink on our chest and keep this day moving", I say as I get out the car.

When we get back I can see that it's way more than the usual crowd outside. People probably felt the need to just get out and get some fresh air today. Karen and Vickie are outside and they never really come out. I've been out with Vickie a few times but that's about it. Just drinks and hugs. She still might feel some type of ay when she see me and Toya, but she really doesn't know anything, all she can do is speculate. Toya already got her assumptions too, so when we get out she says, "there go your girl". I wasn't surprised because that's something females do. When we get towards the door, I separate from Toya and go hug Vickie real quick. She whispers, "she been on yo head since she heard about me, huh? She still not on my level." She tells me to check my phone, and when I get in the building it is her asking if we hanging out today. Toya is standing by the corner of the aisle when I get all the way in. I can see by her facial expression that she got something to say. "You just had to say something to the bitch, didn't you?", she says. "Man, c'mon", I say as we walk towards our areas. Neither one of them can really say shit about anything at the end of the day because it's no title with neither. "I guess she like you too now", Toya says as she goes to her area. I crack a small smile and shake my head as I watch her walk off.

    After I get situated, I reply to Vickie's message. "Right after work?", I ask. "Yes", she sends back. I tell her I will get with her later after work. I see she not gone stop. It's like she has her mind set and that's all she seeing. She doesn't see Toya at all, and really doesn't care.

I see Mack and JP walking past towards their areas, but it looks like JP is crying. Mack comes over after he notices me and says that Larry was JP cousin. They never really let anyone know so people wouldn't think JP got in on some hookup shit. Mack says he knew it already but didn't say shit either. "Damn, I know JP fucked up", I tell Mack. "Larry was his cousin? That's messed up." "He already said he going straight to the bar after work", Mack says. "He said he getting some light for himself and some dark for Larry, since Larry only drunk dark. I told him I'm gone have a round with him then I gotta go get my daughter. I'm gone try and not let him go extra hard, but you know how that shit be. You gotta let people handle certain shit how they handle it. We work tomorrow so he know he gotta get up early, so hopefully that will send him home early. " "Well, just keep an eye on him", I say. "If he good when he leave then he should be good to drive home." "Yeah, I'll keep watch over him", Mack says as he walks off. I can't even imagine what JP going through right now. And then the job not saying nothing makes it look like they didn't give a shit.

The day goes on as usual, even though nothing is seeming usual about this day. Minute by minute, hour by hour, time goes on as if nothing happened. I don't know at this point whether to be mad at the union I pay dues to or the company I work for. Fuck it, it's a combo. They both on the shit list. All they gone do is blame each other anyway, so fuck it, war on both of them. I expect my pre-paid law firm to be on point and have my back in whatever situation, and I expect the company I work for to have some kind of sympathy.

I catch eyes with Vickie while I'm looking up the line and I just stare at her a few seconds, looking her up and down. I guess I'll go hang with her for a little bit after work. I overhear the ladies down from me talking about Kamesha. They say she ended up getting transferred out because she claimed she had chest pains. Not a surprise. It could be serious, but when you cry wolf so much, people don't know what to believe.

I'm sure Toya is probably wondering why I haven't brought her any parts, but I was just waiting until I had enough so I wouldn't have to go back over there. She probably don't even realize it anyway. Knowing her, she back there running her mouth. When I finally get over there, just like I thought, she is talking with Tom. I damn near want to burst out laughing, but I just drop off her parts and make my way back to my area. Toya holler out my name before I get too far. She comes up and says, "so , you wasn't gone say bye? You were just gone leave without a hug or nothing?" "I already told you", I say, "I'm not interrupting nothing. I'll hit you up later. I'm getting ready to leave. You gotta get back to your company anyway." I give her a quick hug and head back to my area. She stands there for a quick second and then heads back to her area.

I get back to my area and look around to make sure everything is in order for the next person when they come in. I text Vickie to see what she got in mind. She tells me to meet her at the gas station and we'll figure it out after that. I got about a two-hour time frame so whatever she got in mind, she gotta make it happen quick.

The bell rings and I make my way towards the door. Toya is walking with Jazz and stops to say bye as I'm walking past. She had to cut across the aisle so I know a few people saw the whole thing. Just the type of shit the paparazzi need to see. I give her another quick hug and she catches up to jazz. "Damn, can I get a hug too?", I hear a voice saying from behind me. I turn around and it's Vickie, with a sarcastic look on her face. "Your girl wanted a hug huh?", she says. "She be on your head though. I see why. I don't blame her." I'm trying to just listen to her without saying nothing because I know she just talking shit. I'll tell her about herself later. I give her a sarcastic smile and continue out the door towards my car. I text her to make sure she going straight to the gas station. I also text Sarah and let her know that I'm making a stop after work. She still won't be home before me so it won't matter. I'll pick up dinner so she won't have to worry about that either. No matter what, no female will ever be her.

When I get to the station, Vickie is parked where she can pull right out once she sees me. she calls and asks if I want some wings. I tell her sure and I follow her after she pulls out. W ride about ten minutes and then pull up at Chicken Shack. Good choice by Vickie. She runs in and grabs the food and runs back to her car without saying anything. Before I can pull up beside her, she is already pulling out the lot. Now I'm wondering where the hell we going. I guess she gone pull over somewhere or something. after riding for a little bit longer though, I see the sign for the freeway. I follow her onto the freeway hoping she not going that far. We going away from my house so that's the only thing about it. My drive back will be a bitch.

Vickie is signaling to exit, and when we finally get to her complex, I realize that I've seen the place before, just in passing. Didn't know anyone that lived in there. Damn, they got a gate and everything. I'm not surprised at her spoiled ass though. We pull around a couple corners and she pulls up to a spot near the end of the road. I pull up beside her after she pulls in the driveway. She waits for a minute then the garage door opens. I pull up behind her when she pulls in. It look like she just moved in because it's boxes stacked up in the garage. She closes the garage and says, "well, this is home". "i still have to organize everything because I only been here for about a month. I'm getting there though." "So, you just be out here chilling, huh?", I ask. "It seem pretty quiet out here." "That's the same thing my dad said when he helped me move in", she says. "I gotta have him come hook up my entertainment system too, since I ain't got no dude." I laugh and say, "yeah, ok., they be all on you though." "But they ain't here, though", she says quickly. "And I'm glad you feel comfortable here, so you won't have a problem when I ask you to come over." She goes in the back in the bathroom but keeps talking. "So you mad you followed me?" "Hell naw", I say as I hear the shower running. When she comes out, she got on some leggings and a t-shirt that barely comes to her waist. Damn, Vickie thick as hell. "I know you fresh off work so you want to get out them clothes", she says. "Here, I got you these." She hands me a bag with a t-shirt and some basketball shorts in it. "I hope everything fits. I picked it out the other day at Foot Locker. I figured you could wear a 3x and the shorts, I asked the guy in the store if they would fit. I got a towel in the bathroom for you so you can get clean right quick. Before I can even say anything she says, "see, I'm on top of everything. I got you all hooked up. When I figured out that I was gone invite you over, I went and got everything. If you would've said no, I would've just kept everything until you finally came over." "Well, what if I said no?", I ask. "Then, I would've just took the stuff back before the receipt expired. But I had a feeling you wouldn't say no, and I was right." i head back towards the bathroom, shaking my head. I can't believe she actually copped all this just so I can be comfortable when I came over here.

After I come out, Vickie has both our plates made, with an unopened bottle of wine on the table. Damn, she don't be bullshitting. I know it took her a minute to set all this up. Yeah, she's a different type of woman, for sure. We finish the food, drink about half the bottle, and chill for a while. After we finish the bottle, I tell her that I have to be going so I can make the drive across town. I give her a hug and tell her I will see her tomorrow.

Chapter: The Day After

I get to work later than usual and the vibe is exactly the same as it was yesterday. It seem like it's extra quiet though. Not like yesterday, but even quieter. Maybe people are still fucked up about the way they handled everything yesterday. I know I am.

I see Paul on the floor speaking to a group of people. This might be the earliest I've ever seen him on the floor, ever. He usually come through right before lunch or a little bit after. He should be here at this time anyway, that's how I feel. The earlier you get to address the problem, the quicker you can get a solution. Mack is standing by the group, but he is hugging another young lady that I don't know. As I get closer, I notice that everybody is crying, or wiping away tears. Mack sees me and immediately comes over and says, "man, I should've stayed there with him". "What happened?", I ask him. He pauses for a quick second and then says JP died in a car accident last night. "He ran a red light and ended up hitting a telephone pole and flipping his car", Mack says. "when the ambulance got there, they found him outside the car. He was pretty much gone before he got to the hospital, his sister said. Crazy part is that she called me from his phone to tell me. I thought it was his ass still out at one in the morning and it was her calling with the news. This shit crazy because I was at the fucking bar *with* him. We left at the same damn time! We had two shots apiece and two Coronas. I know that shit for a fact because I was the one ordering the shit. We got outside and he said he was good. Maybe he stopped somewhere else, I don't know, but when we left, he was good. Then I get the call this morning from his sister. Damn!"

I don't even know if I can even get this shit in my head right now. After everything else that's happened, this tops it off. "Damn JP", I say to Mack. I get ready to start my day and tell Mack I'll holler at him later. This shit is unbelievable. Like a long ass dream the just won't end. I hadn't known JP that long, but it was damn near two years of working with him and damn near talking to him every day. That's fucked up.

I see Ced walking up asking people questions. I guess he heard the latest news. I can tell by the way people are reacting that JP knew a lot of people. He had worked here the longest out of all of us so I'm sure he knew a few people. I wonder if they gone handle this shit the same way they handled everything else. Ced says the he never worked anywhere where people died like this. "This shit new to me man", he says. "We had one person die at my plant, that was it. Well, at least that's all I heard about." "What they do when the person died?", I ask. "They had some counselors come through and talk to a few people, and some people even went home early. The person that died was well=known throughout the plant." Well, you see what they do over here", I say. "Pretty much nothing." "I see", Ced says. "That's the crazy part. They have to realize that people work with each other every day. We here more than we at home, so it's like the people we work with are our family."

Paul is also walking the line, speaking to people as their doing their work. He comes down by me and calls me over to where he is speaking. The line has stopped at this point. He tells us there will be a meeting in a few minutes for the whole area where JP worked to discuss not only JP, but Larry as well. I guess that's a start, more than what they did before. Maybe they didn't know how to handle all of this, but you have to at least speak on a situation when it happens.

As Paul is talking, Michelle is motioning for everyone to meet in the center of the aisle. When we get over there, they tell us they are taking us to a room off the floor to discuss things and just let people express their feelings or whatever. I see Mack on our way to the room and he's going the opposite way. "I'm out man", he says. "I don't even feel like working today, for real. I asked Michelle if I could leave and she said it was fine, so I'm gone. Hit me up later. I'm probably gone just go to the cut and chill. I got a headache from all this shit." I already know how Mack feeling. JP was his closest friend up in here.

We get up to the room and it's not even big enough to hold everyone. As I look around, I see people wiping away tears, and just hugging. It's no specific way you can tell someone how to deal with death, you just have to let them handle it how they choose. I just feel for their families. To lose somebody so sudden, that's crazy.

They bring in a speaker to give people time to voice their opinions and just vent about the situation. I tell the speaker that next time a situation occurs like this, it should be handled a little bit better, and the counselors should be available sooner. It's no way to tell what someone is thinking, but at least have the counselors ready in case they are needed. Paul had mentioned that counselors would be available when Larry died, but no one ever showed

After the speakers are finished, we head back down to the work floor. This is going to be a helluva day, I already can tell. no one feels like working, especially after dealing with these last two days, but we know it's a business and the show must go on.

The whole meeting and everything took us past the first break and damn near to the second break. I get over to Toya to take her some parts and Jazz is over there talking about JP. She says more and more info is coming out about JP's accident. A few people actually saw them talk about it on the news, but they didn't give out the person name because the relatives hadn't been contacted. Jazz says she started with JP so she had been knowing him five years. It's like a tight-knit family, as I said before. And even though we had a discussion about lunchtime before, I still made sure to ask Toya, just to confirm it.

    I'm already set to leave as soon as the lunch bell rings, so I get to the door a little before it rings. We had a lot of downtime with everything going on today. As I'm walking out, I notice that it's a few more people outside than usual. More people than I've ever seen, actually. I guess everybody needed some fresh air. I see Toya and Jazz walking together through the parking lot. I know for sure she didn't mention Jazz earlier when I said something. fuck it. "Where ya'll going?", I holler at them across the parking lot. "We was looking for your car", Jazz says. "And yes, I'm riding with ya'll today, so no quickies today." "What?", you tripping, I say. Jazz starts laughing. "I'm just saying, in case ya'll planned on it, ya'll can wait until later. I need a drink." I can't stop laughing at how crazy Jazz is.

Then I give Toya a look like what the fuck because she must be telling Jazz something. she just shrugs her shoulders like she ain't said shit.

We get to the store and Toya says she got it, so I stay in the car. It's a few more cars than normal at the store so it takes them a little longer to come out. They come out with a half-pint and they kill most of it while we hit a few corners. I have a couple shots out of it but they do the most damage. Jazz starts saying how long she had known JP and how crazy all of this shit is. Yeah, life can be a bitch sometimes. JP was so fucked up from Larry passing that he ended up pretty much killing himself. No one will ever know what actually happened, or how it all played out. Mack was probably the last person to talk to him. Damn.

We pull back up to the job with a few extra minutes left, even with the crowd at the store. I tell Toya that I'm going to sit in the car for a couple minutes so she can go on with Jazz. I text Vickie "when" and text Sarah that I hope her day is going fine. Sarah texts back "fine", and Vickie texts back "tomorrow". As long as Vickie understands my situation, she'll be all right.

I see the medical cart when I get over to my work area, and I'm thinking Kamesha must be going. Shit, she goes damn near everyday so instantly that's the first thing that someone will think. It's messed up, but hey, she can blame herself. Whoever they there for must be laying on the ground because the cart is empty. The line has started by this time so a few people have to scramble to get back to their work stations because they were being nosy. The shit didn't stop nothing either. They still figured out a way to get the line started, even with the medical staff right there. I guess the TL over there jumped on the job. when I look back over there, I see TJ limping to the cart. Hell naw, again? If I got hurt as much as him, they would probably tell me to stay home. Any little thing and he going to medical. I don't know who worse, him or Kamesha. The second half of the day is going at a faster pace than the first half, maybe because all the shit happening. I guess To, finally gave up on Toya, because I been seeing him talking to this same female over the past few days. Not like he hiding it either, so maybe he finally gave up.

Michelle is walking the line, looking at the floor., and it looks like she is looking for something. she gets closer and I can hear her saying "somebody need to cleanup around here." I glance at the floor and really don't see what the big deal is. It's a couple pieces of paper, but nothing major. She looks at me and says, "did you hear me"? "I heard you", I say. "It looks pretty clean to me over here though. Just a few pieces of paper, that's it. " "Well, I see a couple pieces of paper over there", she says. "So make sure you get that up before I come back through here." I watch her walk away, feeling like calling her back to let her know how petty she is, but I just keep quiet. Damn, she don't have to be a bitch all the time. She can take a break every now and then. I know I'm not the only one that feel that way either. Somebody needs to talk to her, for real. I'm not hoping anyone get fired, but she need to be talked to. People have enough stuff to deal with than to come in here and deal with a bullshit supervisor as well. She gone piss the wrong person off and they gone be on her head.

I go back and forth through messages with Vickie to make the rest of the day go by faster. She keep telling me how she can't wait until tomorrow. I guess she got something planned like before. She does have a nice duck=off spot though. Perfect location and not too far to get to.

I get home and kick back on the couch after getting out of my work clothes and hitting the shower. Sarah gets here and I don't even hear her come in. she wakes me up and has some take-out Olive Garden in the stove. Right on time. I meant to call her when I came in earlier to see what we were doing for dinner. Well, that's something I didn't have to worry about today because she was up on it.

Chapter: Clearing The Air

Maybe I'm just anxious or something, but I wake up before my alarm even goes off. Not like this day is supposed to go any different than the rest, but it just feels like it's going to be a great day. I stop for breakfast since I get out earlier than usual, but I get both Toya *and* Vickie something to eat. I know Vickie will be surprised, Toya probably gone act like she knew it was coming. The traffic isn't as heavy because I'm out earlier than usual, so the ride into work is smooth. I get a great parking spot and head on in ready to get this over with.

I stop by Toya's area and she hasn't made it in yet. Perfect. I leave her stuff right by her work station so she can see it when she gets in. when I get back over to my area, Vickie is down at her work station getting situated. I walk down there and give her sandwich, and sure enough, the shit shocked her. She puts it down, gives me a hug, and whispers, "I can't wait till later" in my ear. I walk off smiling to myself.

Michelle is walking the line, I guess to see who is here, and she walks right past without saying shit, once again. I guess some things will never change. No way she can come in here every day and just be in her feelings like this. One day she'll realize it's easier to work with us than try and work against us. She will never get shit done like that.

As I'm getting situated, Toya comes up and says, "hey boo", holding her arms out, waiting for a hug. I don't even mention the sandwich. I'd rather keep it as a surprise to see how she react. She walks off and stops to talk to Jazz on the way to her area. Right before the bell rings I get a text message, thinking it's from Toya, but it's from Vickie. She's just saying thanks again and telling me that it was right on time. I'm pretty sure Toya has seen the sandwich by now, maybe she just busy this morning.

When I finally have to take some parts back to Toya, she is of course talking to her favorite co-worker, Tom. The sandwich isn't where I left it, so I know for sure she ate it, or at least saw it. I say, "what's up" to both of them, grab some empty bins, and head back to my area. No need in asking about the sandwich. If she ate it, fine, if not, then that's fine too. If she thought he brought it, that's also fine.

The day is moving as smooth as ever. No downtime but at least the line is moving at a decent pace and the time is moving fast. We have about a hour before lunch and Toya still hasn't mentioned shit. I've been over there enough that if it was a big deal, she would've said something. Vickie texts me asking if I want some chicken for lunch. I text her back "absolutely". That's what I'm talking about. Hook *me* up sometimes. Toya hasn't said shit about food either so I guess she doing her own thing for lunch. I know I'm not checking to see. She had more than enough time to say or ask whatever and she been quiet the whole morning.

When the bell rings for lunch, I am already at the door waiting. I get to my car and it's still no sign of Toya. After waiting exactly one minute, I pull off without texting or nothing. Toya definitely know the routine and she definitely know I'm not just gone wait. I go to the store and grab me a couple of things and soon as I come out, I hear, "so, it's like that"? I look and see Jazz and Toya getting out of Jazz car. Toya comes up and says, "I meant to tell you I was riding with Jazz today". "Ok", I say nonchalantly as I pull out the parking lot. Still no word on my little good deed from earlier.

I get back and as I'm walking to my work area, I see Vickie walking down towards me. she hands me a bag with my food in it and turns and goes back to her work area, only speaking to a handful of people. You already know she not too friendly. I'm surprised she even brought the food down here. A young lady watches the whole scene a few feet from me, and when Vickie walks away she says, "hell naw", "she don't like nobody, but she definitely like yo ass." "She might owe me that", I said. "Well, she still brought it down to you. I'm telling you, the bitch don't like nobody." I laugh at her statement as I get myself together for the rest of the day.

Toya comes over as I'm getting her parts ready to take to her. "Oh, you ordered food? Wait, how you get food and you was at the store?" "I didn't even buy this", I say. "Somebody got it for me." "Oh yeah, so one of your female friends got you lunch?", she asks.

"I mean, it's just lunch", I say. "Did you get a breakfast sandwich today?" "How you know?", she asks. At this point I don't know if she bullshiting or not. "So you didn't get a sandwich this morning?", I ask her again. "It was a sandwich over there when I came in but I didn't eat it. I threw that shit away. I asked did anybody see who left it and nobody could remember. Tom said he didn't buy it either so I just threw it away." I'm trying o get my words together. She threw it away? "Well, thanks for throwing the shit I brought away", I say. "I was trying to surprise you but you thought some other shit. Didn't even ask me about the sandwich either. Then you say you asked Tom about it. That's even crazier." "Well, you didn't mention it", she says. "After you saw I didn't say nothing, why didn't you say something?", she says. "Why would I mention something that I planned on being a surprise?", I ask. I tell her I'll chat with her later, I have to get back to my work. I'm not even gone bring it up anymore. That's the end of her little breakfast on my end. If she can't figure some simple shit like that out, I'm not gone add to the pressure.

After a few minutes, I get a text from Vickie saying, "I see your boo stopped down there. She still not on my level." I laugh to myself after reading that shit. Vickie is something else. I wonder what she got up her sleeve for today? She had everything on point last time, down to the size. That's some different type shit. Toya wouldn't even know how to put nothing like that together.

Speaking of Toya, I make my rounds to drop off her parts and actually thought about clearing all that shit up from earlier until I saw her running her mouth. I do my usual, drop off my parts, give a nod to both of them, and go on about my business. I guess the shit registered in Toya's mind from earlier, because she comes up as I'm walking off and grabs my arm. "So. You just gone leave?", she asks. "You just gone drop the parts off and that's it?" I'm looking at her confused because it sound like she blaming me. I tell her in a calm way, with a slight grin, "you know I'm not pulling no number to talk to you. all day today it's been the same shit every time I came over here. Maybe you need to just holler at me outside of work because you too busy up in here. You ain't got the time to discuss nothing in here. I know ya'll females love attention but damn, is the shit that serious? So, I'm gone let you finish talking and not be a hater or a blocker, cause' that's not what I do. I'll probably call you later or something, I don't know." I can tell she is pissed when I walk off, but she should know me by now.

The rest of the day seems like it's flying by. I get a text from Vickie with her address, right before the last bell. I knew the place, I just didn't remember the exact location. As I get outside, I get a text from Toya asking what am I about to do. I guess she saw me walking across the lot. I don't even respond to the message. Nope, not today. She killed it already for herself for today.

When I get to Vickie's apartment, she is already there. Damn, I only made one quick store run. She couldn't have stopped for nothing. I guess she came straight here. Before I can get out the car I get another text from Vickie saying the door is open. When I get inside, I can hear the water running in the shower. I guess Vickie getting freshened up or whatever. She comes out with just a towel on saying I can get in now. It took me a couple seconds for what she was saying to register. I get up and walk right past her as she's drying off her legs, giving her a light smack on the ass as I walk in the bathroom. When I come out, Vickie calls me back to her room where she is laying on the bed in the same thing she came out the shower in, nothing. She asks me to come put some lotion on her and turns over on her stomach. I laugh to myself while walking over to the bed, still drying off. I look Vickie up and down while putting the lotion on my hands. She is definitely one hundred percent grown woman. I remember how smooth her skin was the first time when I start rubbing on her back. I also make sure to pay extra attention to her ass cheeks. I chill at Vickie's for a little over an hour then head home. I text Sarah and tell her I'll grab something for dinner. I get home, relax on the couch and set my alarm just in case I nod off.

Over the next few months, I find myself spending more time with Vickie and less with Toya. Toya still cool and we still hang out every now and then, but I see she gotta have her fan club. Regardless of what she says, she love the fans. I just can't be one of them, really. So we keep it simple at work now. Mack ended up going out on medical after JP died, but he's back and finally getting back to his normal self. You can't really put a timeframe on that shit, so I hit him up every once in a while, to check on him and shit while he was out. Just to try and keep his mind on other shit.

Michelle is still the supervisor, so you know it's still days where her attitude is ridiculous, and days where it seems like you're dealing with a different person. Doesn't matter how much I try and stay out her way, she makes it her business to say something to me. Ced is still the TL too. He even knows when people like to have their breaks throughout the day. Yeah, it ain't shit, but his ass comes in handy when somebody want a break.

Everybody that started with me is full-time now. Full benefits, profit sharing, vacation time, and paid=time-off. It was a few people that hadn't been rolled over to full-time but they eventually got rolled over too. It's now a new group of TPT's that came in after us that are still waiting to be rolled over, so we try and keep them encouraged and in good spirits. Paul is still our steward but he has been extra busy lately because the company is tightening up on the attendance policy, resulting in many people getting time off or being in the attendance program. The steward is like our lawyer, he ain't no damn savior. We have to be smarter and control what we can control. Over the time I've been here, I've learned to take care of myself and be responsible for my own actions. At the end of the day, that's the only thing you can do. You can't rely on anyone to have your back like yourself. Toya had to learn the hard way.

Chapter: Changes

We had been hearing about and seeing people fall victim to the attendance policy, and had ben joking about being taken upstairs, but never really thought that day would come. Toya had mentioned that she had a doctor's appointment and I told her to let Paul know ahead of time so she wouldn't have to deal with it later. Toya didn't have any proof that she had an appointment because it was mad over the phone, so she called in instead and brought her paperwork in the next day. The problem was that her appointment was at twelve in the afternoon. The company felt that she should have came into work and then asked to leave. That really didn't seem like a reasonable choice to me because they always claim to have a manpower issue at my job. why come in knowing you might not be able to take care of your business?

After everything was said and done, Toya ended up getting written up and missing two days. The few people who knew the situation didn't understand how that could happen. Most people blamed Paul for letting it happen in the first place. Even though we weren't as close as we used to be, the shit had me kind of angry too. I felt like she didn't get a fair trial by being suspended. No way should a person be suspended when they have the right paperwork.?

Every three years there is an election held where employees vote on various positions, from the Local President to the stewards that represent various departments. I'm not even sure who running for most of the positions because I've only dealt with Paul. It's not like I interact with anyone else on the regular, so whoever plan on running need to show their face. Shit, Paul need to show his face more, actually. From what I heard, a lot of people feel like he could be doing better. I haven't needed him in my defense on anything, but from what I hear, it's best to be prepared yourself.

In the short time I've been working here, I've met a lot of people and learned how to deal with people on different type of levels, from the assembly level to the corporate level. Most people say they like how I always voice my opinion and stand up for what I think is right. Vickie even joked with me one day about running for something. I thought about it, even talked with Sarah about it too. I was laid back and feeling out the scene when I first started, and now I'm getting used to more and more people and learning new things about how this union thing works.

Running for a position doesn't seem like something that's hard to do. Winning is what I think is the hard part. You have to have that connection with people that will allow them to gain your trust and feel that you will do the right thing. Popularity helps, but honesty is more important. Anybody can be popular, but not everyone is honest. The Toya incident really let me know that it was time for a change. No way should a person be suspended when they take care of everything they can handle. Paul's advice for Toya was that it was over his head. That was a sign that whoever is in charge needs to be replaced. I don't know what situation or position would be best for me, but I'll do my research and talk to a few people and figure that out. Fuck it, I'm running for something.

The End

Made in the USA
Lexington, KY
14 August 2017